Lest we forget: The Dead, the Dying and Those Laid to Rest

By G. C. Dark

Copyright © 2024, Griffin Conway

No part of this publication may be reproduced, distributed, or transmitted in any form or by any means, including photocopying, recording, or other electronic or mechanical methods, without the prior written permission of the publisher, except in the case of brief quotations embodied in critical reviews and certain other noncommercial uses permitted by copyright law.

All rights reserved

Lest we forget: The Dead, the Dying and Those Laid to Rest

Copyright © 2024, Griffin Conway

Sagittarius Heart Publishing 2024

ISBN: 979-8-9879384-3-0

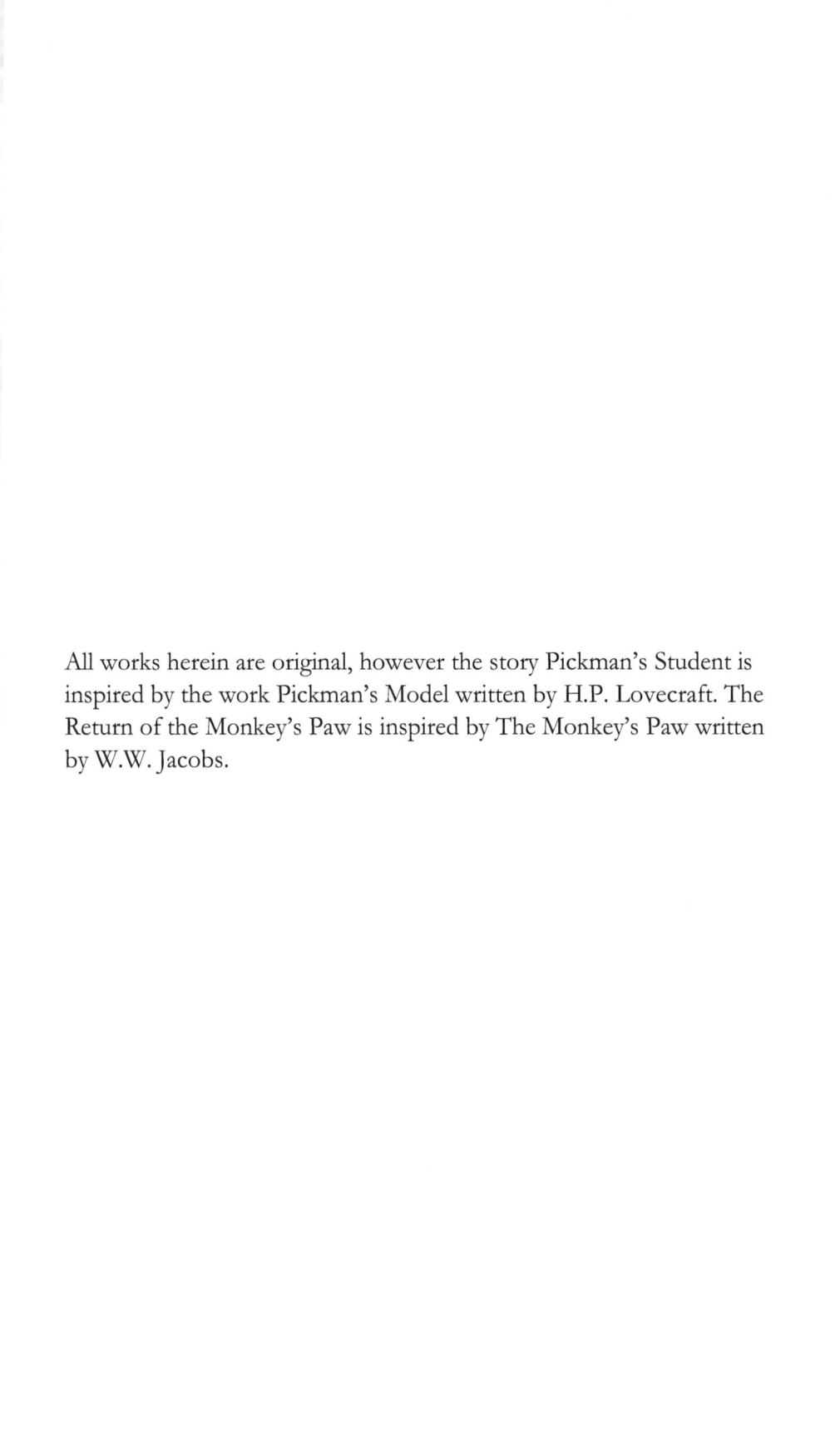

All works herein are original, however the story Pickman's Student is inspired by the work Pickman's Model written by H.P. Lovecraft. The Return of the Monkey's Paw is inspired by The Monkey's Paw written by W.W. Jacobs.

Table of Contents

Servant of the Blood 1
    I 2
    II 8
    III 11
    IV 13
    V 15
    VI 18
    VII 23
    VIII 27
Tales from Obscura 31
Walkers 32
    I 33
    II 41
    III 49
Giger City 59
Pleasant Falls 74
    I 75
    II 82
    III 94
Poezie de Groaza 102
    I 103

II	106
III	109
IV	113
V	118
VI	122
It Wakes	126
Rending the Veil	133
I	134
II	138
III	144
IV	151
San Tino 88	153
I	154
II	158
Pickman's Student	161
I	162
II	166
III	170
IV	177
The Return of the Monkey's Paw	180

BOOK 1:

Servant of the Blood

I

His body shook as he hunched over the bathroom sink in pain. His stomach seized as he spat up blood and saliva thick with bone marrow. He took a look at himself in the mirror and saw long strings of milky red sinew hanging from his mouth. Spitting it out in disgust, he threw his hand on the shower taps and turned the water on. Stripping down, he sat down against the cold tile bathtub as the hot water ran over his naked form. He closed his eyes as he tilted his head up to meet the water.

Flashes ran through his mind that caused him to jolt his eyes open, horrible flashes, the things he'd done and that had been done to him. He placed his head in his hands as he began to cry.

A night ago, he was walking home when the thing caught him. It clawed at his stomach and tackled him to the ground. Soon he felt a stinging bite to his neck before a cold chill ran through his body. He overturned on his side and began to throw up and soil himself. The thing ran off into the night.

Benjamin Holden or Ben to his friends was man no more. He died that night; he felt his body ache, his flesh burn and his blood boil. He felt like he had worms inside him and he died.

His bright blue eyes faded to a cold grey, and then he sat up. He felt what should have been the cool night air, but he wasn't cold. He heard voices and sounds that came from everywhere and nowhere; he seemed to move faster and more fluidly – he had been reborn. Then he felt it.

That stinging urge deep in his stomach. The hunger. That savage need to feast. Benjamin spent that night trying to eat, but with every mouthful of food, from steak to eggs to peanut butter, hamburgers and fries – he couldn't choke it down. He spat it out in disgust. His stomach howled in hunger, and he felt light headed, dizzy and floating. In frustration, he left his apartment and went back out into the night, his head throbbing, his vision blurred and all around him seemed like chaos. Every noise was thundering and echoing in his mind as if he was in a cavern a thousand feet down, and a hellfire storm of brimstone-rain rocketed around him.

His hands shook as every sight, and sound overwhelmed him. Finally, out of exhaustion, Benjamin threw himself into an alley and started to throw up bile, the stomach acid burning his esophagus. He shook violently before he seemed to fall into a sort of coma.

It was the smell of coffee that woke him. The chill of the alley and street was gone. Benjamin's eyes opened as he looked around the unfamiliar apartment. Modern in décor and style, he slowly sat up on the olive-green sectional sofa. A blanket had been placed over him.

"Good morning," a soothing, friendly voice echoed off the walls and only hurt his ears for a few seconds. His eyes adjusted as the frame of a woman sat across from him, placing a coffee cup down. Weakly he laid back down. "Who…where am I?"

"Well, I saw you having a fit. I'm a nurse and I thought you were having a seizure. It was so late. I figured if you had any real medical issues, I could get you into a hospital bed faster than anyone else. My name is

Ela, Ela Kennedy." She smiled softly as she placed a coffee cup down in front of him.

Benjamin's eyes and body hurt. He felt as if he had been stung by a million bees, waves of discomfort rushing over him. He felt his body throb as he covered his face with the blanket.

"You should probably get some sleep; I checked your wallet, Benjamin Holden." Her tone was enthusiastic and warm. "Your cell phone and wallet are on the kitchen counter. You can help yourself to a shower if you need it or call someone if you need to. I don't expect you to stay here, but I told my neighbor that I had a friend staying with me, and if you leave, just let her know to lock the door."

From under the dark of the blanket, Benjamin responded, "Why are you doing this? I'm a stranger." His tone was low and slow, somewhat slurred.

Ela stood up and took a sip of coffee, her hand instinctively touching the small silver cross necklace she wore as she smiled. "Well Benjamin – or Ben? If I can. Jesus saves and he helped all kinds of people, and Florence Nightingale did too. Both of them would've done what I did, and so I did what I did because that's what they would have liked. Anyway, there is food in the fridge and you are welcome to a shower. I have to go work a shift but I'll be back tonight. I gave you some fluids and a shot or two to help with the spasms you were going through, so you should be ok at least until I get back."

Benjamin let out a strained "thank you" before he fell back into the deep realms of a medicated sleep. Ela Kennedy smiled as she grabbed her keys and left the suffering man to his recovery.

Strange haunted dreams plagued Benjamin Holden as he slept, a chemical haze of some odd memory, a dark recollection of sorts. The snarling sound of a hound, the odor of raw meat, stinging and tearing, the sound of something lapping up thick stew or wet chunks of meat. Benjamin burst from this dream as he stumbled to the floor. His eyes no longer hurt. His head no longer throbbed. The hunger still remained in his gut. He shakily stood and walked to a window. Peeking out of the curtain, he saw the night had fallen across the city. He sat himself down at the table and saw a cold cup of coffee in front of him. Benjamin didn't know what to make of his condition. He gripped his stomach in pain as he hurried back to the kitchen and tried to find food. Same as before in his apartment, trying to choke down any of these fruits or meats would not work. Frustrated and confused, Benjamin returned to the living room and turned on the television to the nightly news.

"More bodies found near Chase Park. They appear to have been attacked and…I'm sorry to say this but there is no other way – savaged – as if by some sort of animal." Benjamin turned off the television as a memory raced to his mind. Chase Park was where he was attacked…or was that a dream. Had anything happened at all?

As he thought this, the sound of a thunderous scraping following by tumblers falling into place blasted through his ears. His head turned toward the door as Ela Kennedy stepped back into her home. Upon seeing him sitting up, Ela smiled. "Hey Benjamin, how are you doing?"

Benjamin smiled and laid back "Better, thank you. How are you? How was work?"

She shrugged as she placed her bag on the table. "The last few nights I've been having to treat a lot of victims of the Chase Park attacks. It's gotta be some sort of bear or wolf. Anyway, you wouldn't mind if I took a hot shower really fast, would you?"

Benjamin shook his head. "Not at all. It's your home after all." Suddenly, he caught wind of her, her scent, and from somewhere deep he thought he heard her heart beat. As he thought this, he heard her voice trail off, "I won't be a minute," and then the sound of water. Benjamin slowly stood up and followed her. Peering into her bedroom, he saw the light of the bathroom and a shadow as Ela slipped into the shower. His heart began to race. He could smell her sweet skin. He heard every water droplet hitting her flesh. Benjamin's eyes turned a pale grey as he heard a heartbeat swell in his ears. Suddenly, the water turned off, but Benjamin couldn't move; the heart beat and her scent was too strong and he was caught in a trance.

She opened the door and let out a startled noise. "Benjamin! I think you should wait outside…what's wrong?" Her voice was a million miles off. She saw Benjamin standing there, his grey eyes almost twinkling. He was breathing heavy and almost wheezing, a long single strand of saliva hanging from his chin. As she went to move, Benjamin allowed the hunger to dictate its dark whisper, a dark and carnal voice from inside. The hunger had been speaking to him all this time and now he fully understood what it meant.

He pounced on her with such speed, she knew not what to do. As she screamed, she felt a piercing sting on her arm and started to let out a howl of horror. Benjamin had sunk his fangs into her arm and was sucking her blood as he was ripping chunks of her flesh away. He covered her mouth and began to eat.

Savaging the feast, Benjamin gnawed on Ela's body and bones. He spent half an hour dismembering her and consuming her flesh and bone marrow, her blood sinking into the carpet as Benjamin allowed himself to indulge in this dark whisper, this demonic hunger.

He had grabbed her breast and all but ripped it off. He had consumed half of her face along with several bite marks along her legs and arms; her blood drained.

Now, Benjamin sat in the shower and glanced over to the remains of Ela Kennedy.

A euphoric wave of guilt and lustful satisfaction washed over him. The hunger had been reduced to a small growl in the back of his mind – this he could not ignore.

Benjamin had to be realistic about what he had seen and gone through. What he had done – Benjamin knew he was no longer human. He knew he was a murderer, a devil of that old hellfire pit.

Benjamin was now something out of time and beyond the reach of any god or creator's love. He had been taken out of the food chain and placed somewhere else, above humans and people. For if the lion feasted on the gazelle, so would Benjamin feast on the human.

Benjamin Holden died that night in Chase Park, and something much older, much darker and with an insatiable hunger and urge had taken root in Benjamin's body.

II

Candlelight danced off the walls as the sound of pacing footsteps echoed around the room. The young man with a bible in hand read verses and chapters, and every now and then, a crimson teardrop would wet the page he was reading. He threw himself down in a pew and looked to Jesus on the cross before standing again and kneeling at the cross. "Why have you seen fit to plague me so?" His tone was pathetic and weak. "Was I not loved enough? Did I not pray enough? Was my faith not enough?" His pleas were that of the final few hours of desperation.

"God created man to live and love, to follow the light. Did God create the contagion to fell man? Lord, I have killed and fed off many of your children. Have you not made me a murderer? Am I not a sinner? Is killing not a sin, and yet I must kill to thrive in the proper way? Am I not a creature of some ageless pit? Have I not seen eon after eon and yet only a sunrise from movies? My life is condemned to the dark. I am loved by the moon and her stars. Lord, I haven't been part of your plan for eons. Who is to blame?"

The vampire wrapped his arms around the statue of Christ as he held tight. "Forgive me Lord. For all I have done is to thrive, and yet I should not be allowed to live."

Isaiah looked to the statue of the savior and saw tears. "You weep with or for me?"

Isaiah felt a sting as he recoiled from the hug and clutched his hands. The stigmata had formed, a deep sigh of relief crossing Isaiah's face as he looked to the statue. "Yes, Lord."

Isaiah stood to his feet and removed his cloak and black jeans; his tanned, nude form would've been flawless had it not been for the deep cuts and scars. "Blood is the life and so blood back to the creator." Isaiah walked to the front pew and grabbed a black bag that had been in the room. Isaiah reached in and pulled out a well-used cat-o-nine-tails. Isaiah grabbed one of the many candles in the room and tilted his head back as he let the wax drip down his body. He made the holy symbol in wax on his chest as he returned the candle to its place. Grabbing the cat, Isaiah lashed his back; with every slash and lash, he shed blood and flesh.

This ritual had been done a million times. He had gotten good at it. He felt the nails and spikes tear into his skin. The tips had been rubbed in garlic and holy water to prevent healing. The blood ran thick and black as Isaiah kept eye contact with the weeping statue, and as the statue cried tears, Isaiah cried blood.

He had spent one thousand years on this planet as a child of the night, a plague, the night walker.

Every culture had them; every culture knows them.

Vampire.

He had fed on man, woman, child, animal. He had fed on the wicked, the unborn babe from the sleeping mother. He had laid entire households to rest. He had seen days turn to weeks and weeks to years and years to history and history to forgotten knowledge. Isaiah was a follower of Christ. He had seen the new world become the old world. He had seen the dark ages fade to the reconstruction. He dined with the French king and his wife. He dined with the roundheads, and when the new world had begun to develop, he was there. Isaiah saw the shot heard 'round the world, and he was there to see the war to end all wars and the war after that.

A lifetime was more than he had ever wanted, and now he would give himself to the light, to the sun and light of all lights. His time had finally come — for living as a monster, living as the walking plague, he could no longer do.

Isaiah stared into the face of the statue as he finally dropped the cat which now had chunks of his flesh and blood stuck to it. Isaiah looked out to the great stained-glass windows and saw the earliest rays of dawn. Exhausted, he threw open the large oak doors and kneeled as he spread open his arms, blood-tears streaming down his face as he felt the first warmth, the rays of sun edging over the church roof.

He felt the world become warmer. For the first time in a lifetime, Isaiah felt the sun. Far distant memories flooded his mind, memories of youth and love, memories of humanity. Memories he forgot he forgot. He felt his skin and soul warm to an uncomfortable level as the sun crested over the church. Isaiah let out pained screams as he forced himself to stay on his knees with his arms outstretched. The wax cross caught fire as Isaiah let out a hellish, pained scream. His body caught fire. His hands and arms began to char. His hair started to ash as his skin peeled away.

Black blood began to run. As his blood was exposed to sunlight, it ashed and blew away. Isaiah opened his eyes and was instantly blinded by the sun. His eyes turned to grey and then blew away as dust. Suddenly, the screaming stopped, and all that remained was an ash statue of the creature formerly known as Isaiah.

III

The moon shone over the black valley and washed over the count. He sat in his courtyard amongst the hedgerows as he stared long into the dark. His tall, thin pale form could have been crafted by Bernini. His eyes shimmered in the moonlight. He was nude and once again caught in what he called "The Great Contemplation." His mouth was stained red with fresh blood, and against his ivory, skin color, it looked even more shocking.

At his feet laid the corpse of a woman. She was drained of all her blood, all that would make her, all that she had – her memory, her love and passion, her lust, fear, doubt, her strength. She was nothing more than corpse-rot.

Count Octavian Servius sat in silence as his mind wandered through the ages of time and history. The devil had taken root in his heart and turned it into a living, beating flesh-thorn. He felt the deep satisfaction and in his own way, love. He loved what he was and what he became. With every life he took, with every drop of blood stolen and locked away inside his immortal body, he felt a rush of lust and hate and aimed it directly at the high heavens.

In the ages before the ages, Count Octavian Servius was a prince. He was a king. He was a leader of men…at least he was born to be. His family were a long line of roman leaders, thinkers. Ancient history claims, or at least one point claims that his bloodline was in direct relation to Romulus and Remus; however, this was lost to time and war. Octavian had been born a noble, a leader, a fighter and warrior, a champion of the spear, a gift from the Gods with a blade. He had waged blood war. History breaks empires. It breaks men, kills Gods and buries everything else.

Octavian had seen his fate on the battlefield. As he lay dying, his young, strong body clinging to life, a dark god, a demon, a vision from beyond, the last fading blink of the old gods came to him and bestowed a gift and a curse, an ageless power to bring about the end and death of history and time, to crush and vanish the modern god, any who would follow the undead, a living death. Octavian accepted, and when the final god had died, the young man rose among the dead and walked through the crimson field into the world and whatever history awaited.

The one Christian God now seemed to rule over the land, and so, in spite of him, to spite him and to do all he could in his power to tear down those fake pearly gates and the fool's gold streets, Octavian would stalk and tear one by one, the followers of the fake god.

Standing, the beast walked to a fountain and cleaned his mouth; he looked to the sky and laid another royal curse on the faith. As he walked back to a section of statues, he took hold of a cross and sword and made a warrior's expression, a flash of fury and triumphant victory. He felt the sun on his back. He tightened his grip on the sword and cross as the sun broke over the black sky and turned it into a baby blue. By the rays of the morning sun, all that was left was the corpse-rot of a woman, and several feet away was a stone statue of a young nude warrior prince from a forgotten time in history.

IV

The gentle sound of water lapping against old, weathered wood was drowned out by the winds and waves. The decaying vessel swayed to and fro in the Obsidian Sea. Standing on deck of this driftwood castle was a single soul, an aged, old mariner. His hands were long and thin. His frame was weak and bony. His eyes reflected the length and depth of the ocean itself. On this aged ghost ship, he alone was king, a haunted existence brought about by the loves and losses, by the time and history that came and went before his eyes. The old mariner had long since said his goodbyes to the world. He was no longer a part of it, nor did he care for whatever was to be found in any society.

He was something else. His were the stories of lore, of history, and now his only friend, the only thing he connected with and that he felt connected to was the sea itself. At one time, he was a man, a prouder sailor, a fisherman, a whaler, a captain, a pirate. His life had always been one of sea. It was fitting that his un-life should be the same.

Weak-willed and broken, the mariner immortal watched over the night. His gaze was staring at everything and nothing, for there was nothing he hadn't seen.

His body seared with a burning and yearning hunger, an urge, a fire to feed, and yet the mariner had not feasted in a lifetime. He had no love for blood, no love for death. He had no love for life and no reason to cater to any of the whims of body or mind. His was an existence of waves, storms and sea-faring tales of old.

The only peace he knew was moments like this. The sun was long since asleep. The eyes of the world had shut. His haunted dreams of the centuries faded, and he was able to just exist. The mariner had taken this old ship that was once full of life and adventure. The wood had been charred in fires. The decks had been baptized in fish and whale blood. The masts were strong. You could almost hear the echo of the sea shanties and drunken bets echo off the walls. Now it was nothing more than a floating tomb with a lone passenger, out of time, out of place and out of the way.

The vampire's eyes scanned those black long waves for anything and yet nothing. The sun would be up soon and when it was, the mariner would retire to the below decks, back into the ghastly sleep, to the memories of his human life, of his lost loves, lost battles, of his childhood, of the night he turned. Of motorcars and sky machines, the last of the world he had known.

He had seen some large metal ships, huge hulking masses of craftsmanship that would shrink even the largest of sea beast to that of a guppy. This was of much of the modern world that he knew. Death could come at the hands of man, rogue wave, sudden fire or storm. The mariner cared not. As was the sea so full of life underneath and yet empty above, so was the mariner who left life's love and the sun for the kiss of the dark and embrace of the night. The world beyond is nothing more than a tale to be told, and a life at sea is both his blessing and curse, for mortal man does mortal things, and the immortal self hungers for both worlds yet condemned to eternal isolation.

V

Dr. Lilian Grace sat at her desk, eyes hurting, head throbbing. Her insides felt cramped and hot. She had already thrown up two times and a third was on the way.

The night shift at the hospital was in full swing, but Dr. Grace was overseeing one patient, a young boy with a rare blood disorder. The chances were, he wouldn't make it through the night. His fight had been going on for weeks now. The family had been in and out seeing him, praying for him, asking every question they could.

Modern medicine seemed to be failing. At the end of the day, it was a fifty-fifty shot. Dr. Grace knew this. She ran tests, took samples. She sent the case out. The options were running thin. All they could do now was wait and watch. The hour was late. The boy's family had left, and she had resigned herself to keep watch over his vitals. His young body heaved with every shallow, labored breath. His skin was pale. His temperature was high.

Dr. Grace sat there, watching him for fifteen minutes, before she returned to her office to look over his charts and tests. Maybe there was something she missed. Maybe there was some note, some reference, something that could help give insight to the cure or at least a way to combat and stabilize him.

It was here where she had thrown up. Her body began to burn. She had been wearing herself down. Lilian Grace now allowed herself to let her guard down. She snapped her blinds shut and took her glasses off to rub her eyes. Lilian had lost patients before; it was hand in hand with the trade. People live and people die, and at the end of the day, sometimes a doctor, a test, a surgery, a cure, pill, vial or prayer won't save you. People die.

Dr. Grace had a lifelong quest to stamp out disease. She had lost her mother and father to a bad case of vermin brought disease. She had seen villages tormented by insect brought plague. She had seen waterborne ailments panic modern metropolises of man. She had seen virus and bacteria spread throughout the world, jumping from plane to flea to rat to person.

The world was wrought with pestilence. It was covered in plague and germ spawn, and there were only so much people could do.

The searing, stabbing pain brought Dr. Grace back to her thoughts. She leaned back in the chair and held her stomach as she violently bent over and, for a third time, threw up in her wastepaper basket. She needed sleep. She needed food. She needed to know that her young ward was going to make it. Dr. Grace needed these things, and yet one was dependent on the other. First and foremost was saving the young life. Then sleep and food would come easy.

All these thoughts ran through her mind as she staggered toward her cabinet, and sliding it open, took out a small black zippered bag, quickly unzipping it. Dr. Grace took out a syringe and began to tie her arm off. Finding a vein, she injected herself with the contents of the needle and fell back into a relaxed state.

Heaven bliss filled her body. Her thoughts calmed and searing pains and jitters came to a sudden halt. Dr. Lilian Grace slowly stood up and adjusted her hair. She threw the needle away and placed the bag back into the cabinet before leaving her office. Renewed energy, less tense and more focused, Dr. Lilian Grace returned to her patient. She stared at the young boy who was now somehow resting easily. Pity filled her eyes. A longing to rid the world of these diseases filled her heart. This was her passion. Suddenly, the boy seized up and his heart stopped.

The life alert alarm triggered, and a small medical team rushed in. Lilian Grace was barking orders as they tried to revive the boy. His heart had simply given out. Nothing could be done.

At exactly three twenty-three in the morning, they called it and Lilian wiped a tear away from her cheek. She steeled her heart as she walked away and back into her office. She had a phone call to make.

Science had failed, and now it seemed to echo and shout louder for her as well.

The final human had died, and with it, proper food was off the menu. Dr. Lilian Grace knew that the world was on a timer now. Food was going to be very scarce, and dark days were ahead. She looked to her cabinet of blood supplies, and in her head did math of how long she could last.

The world would end in a horrible long famine, a bloodless death to an entire race of deathless, to those who could not walk in the sun, those who feasted on blood to survive, those who squandered the humans down to the final million, the final ten thousand and now the final one.

The counter had started, and now vampire kind would know such a terrible end that it would surely sink and destroy, leaving only plants and animals to reign over the ruins of the vampire history, made of blood from the human empire that fell to the cursed kin of the night.

VI

Bonfire light bounced off the trees and jungle thicket. The sound of chanting and tribal drums joined in with the nightly animal and insect chorus of the jungle. Tonight was a ritual, a coming of age. The formerly young men now became blooded warriors. They became men. To the center of a ring surrounded by bonfires, three captives were brought to their knees, their hands and feet bound by vines, their weapons placed in front of them. The tribe created a circle of shield and spear as the captives were cut loose and allowed to stand and take arms. The three young men stepped into the circle, bare-handed, and looked across to their game. To the death. If the captives won, they were allowed to go free and marked as blooded warriors who bowed and worshiped no one. Otherwise, their heads would serve as trophies, and their bodies were cast into the flame.

The chanting and stomping stopped as the elder of the tribe held up his sword which signaled the start of the ritual.

With a sudden flash of anger and fury, the young men raced to meet the captives.

The youngest of the men, his name roughly translated into Snake Fang, ran to meet the armed captive. Carefully choosing his footing and which side to start the attack, he charged in on the captive's left side, narrowly missing the point of the spear that was thrust toward him. Snake Fang got in close and grabbed the spear to begin to wrestle it away from the captive. A strong headbutt caught Snake Fang off guard as he stumbled back for a moment, catching himself and again moving to avoid the spear tip.

Snake Fang had fury in his eyes as his heart filled with a fire from the pit. A rage set over him and Snake Fang charged. As the spear was thrust again, Snake Fang slid under it and targeted the captive's legs. Hooking his right arm around the left leg of the captive, Snake Fang dragged him to the ground and landed a hard punch to the captive's chest. As the captive was dragged down, Snake Fang jammed his thumbs into the captive's eyes and began to slam his head against the cold, hard ground. Snake Fang went wild with a blood lust. His heart was that of a leopard. His anger was that of a spirit.

Within moments, Snake Fang was standing, his body covered in blood as the limp body of a captive laid to rest.

During this time, at the start of the ritual, a young man, whose translated name is Large Rock or Unmovable Boulder, charged in to meet his challenge. The well-built and muscular youth was met with two cuts to his shoulder. The pain and injury were worth the risk. Getting in close, Unmovable Boulder grabbed the captive by the waist and hurled him into the air. As the captive landed on the ground, Unmovable Boulder scrambled to mount the captive, letting out a tribal scream that seemed to shake the very earth. Large Rock unleashed a flurry of ground pounding fists into the face and body of the captive.

In fear and anger, the captive was flailing wildly before his hand found the sharp tip of his dagger, grabbing it and jamming it into Unmovable

Boulder's shoulder, causing a pained fury scream from the warrior youth. The captive scrambled out and moved behind Unmovable Boulder. He tried to get him in a choke hold, but Unmovable Boulder had torn the dagger out, and just as the captive was going in for a choke, he felt a searing pain in his leg. He looked down to see a dagger that was driven down to the bone, sinking to one leg. The captive stared up at Large Rock. As he went to wrench the dagger out, Large Rock grabbed the captive's neck, and with a quick and sudden sick sound, snapped it like a twig. Unmovable Boulder then tossed the limp body aside.

The third of the warrior youth was titled Prince, for he was indeed the son of the Elder. He had to win this fight in order to show he was truly man enough to take his father's throne and lead the tribe.

Walking slowly toward the captive, their fight happened at the same time Snake Fang and Unmovable Boulder had theirs.

Prince beat his chest twice and stared right into the eyes of the captive. It was an unwritten custom that the prince had to showboat a little to show off for the tribe and his father, showing that he always had confidence.

The captive was also a prince of his tribe, the now beaten tribe who lived across the river. These two tribes had long since been at war. Prince stood looking at the captive prince; and for the smallest of moments, the briefest of seconds, a mutual understanding was reached. Prince ran to the captive as the captive took a defensive stance.

Prince was met with a shield and sword; the captive was smart and skillful.

Prince took the defensive stance of his challenge to give himself time to think. He sized up his captive's stance, his grip on the sword and shield, his speed, any opening, any chance to take advantage of the overconfidence of the prideful captive.

During these calculations, Snake Fang and Large Rock moved the bodies of their fallen quarry to the sides. Unmoved by this, the captive prince and Prince kept their eyes locked; each was waiting for the other to make a mistake, a blunder. Any slight distraction would do.

Suddenly, Prince's insight came into focus. They had spent so much time waiting, so much time planning. The captive would never expect the most basic of movements. Rushing in directly at the shield, Prince charged with the speed and power of a boar.

The captive held his shield and readied his sword, thinking this was the mistake. As the captive went to stab outward, Prince swung to the side of the shield and blade, getting inside the range of the sword. The captive pulled back, but not before Prince had landed two punches to the captive's rib cage. The side of the shield rattled Prince's head as he took a few steps back. The captive winced but shook it off just in time to see Prince charging at the shield again. Using the direct blind spot to his advantage, Prince went to slide under and catch his opening again. The captive prince knew this now, and this time simply backed up before readjusting. Prince was waiting for this moment.

Advancing with the backup, Prince moved faster and faster, before he finally grabbed the shield and started to shake it. The captive prince tried to fight against it and use momentum. Prince made himself another opening that landed him two more punches to the captive's side.

Prince then backed up to ready for another attack.

The warrior captive let rage make his decision and charged at Prince. The sharp blade thrusted out of the tiny window, and Prince was able to read and dodge this attack before any damage could be dealt.

The captive prince let out a warrior cry as Prince replied with his own savage scream backed with an animalistic snarl.

Prince rushed in, and this time as the captive thrusted out the sword, prince grabbed hold of the captive's wrist. Dragging the shield arm down the sword arm, Prince then jammed his double-clenched hold into the chin of the captive. Prince wrenched the shield and sword free of the captive, and suddenly shoved his hand into the captive's mouth.

Wrenching down hard, Prince used his other hand and shoved a finger deep into the eye socket of the shocked and dazed captive.

Prince released the captive who stumbled back, and before he could regain his senses, Prince was on top of him with a vine around his throat. Prince pulled back hard, and as the vine snapped, so did the windpipe of the captive. Prince stood up and let out a wild savage howl.

The chanting from the tribe reached to the high night heavens as the fires danced.

The elder called the tribe to order as he stepped down and cut his chest. The blood ran from his chest, and he marked Snake Fang, Large Rock and Prince as blooded warriors.

Then he raised his hand and let it drop.

The end of the ritual saw Snake Fang, Unmovable Boulder and Prince suddenly feasting on the corpses of the recently fallen victims, their bones and flesh and blood consumed by the savage tribal vampires.

VII

The burning incense made the large room smell of lavender and mint along with several other mixed herbs. Prayers and hushed praises quietly made their way from one person to the next.

The ancient city was in the grip of some vicious plague. Rats squeaked and chittered as the decay made its way from flea to human. The water supply had become tainted, and now citizens fell by the wayside, common place death in the once great site of the knowledge and wealth.

The high priests said their prayers. They burned their herbs and used their holy waters to cleanse the wounds and bodies of the great unwashed, who now sought shelter in the grand temple.

The beating of a single drum marked her return. Attention snapped to the center alter as a tall black woman dressed in gold and silver looked out to the flock of people. She stood almost shining in her rare stones. Her gold chains and silver rings seemed to be made of sun and moonlight. Her dark chocolate-esque skin seemed to be crafted from the most flawless piece of obsidian stone.

She stood in silence as the crowd looked on her awestruck. It almost seemed as if the disease could not touch her; dare it would not soil her garments or skin.

The high priestess stepped down from the alter and walked down into the mass of the great unwashed.

She could smell, despite the burning cure-alls, that decay and filth had made its way into the temple.

The priestess looked down to a small frail, bodied child as she cupped his head in her hands. She placed her lips to his forehead and whispered a prayer. The body fell silent and into a deep sleep. The sores and wounds on his face began to slowly heal and vanish as his labored breathing seemed to calm.

The child's mother quickly bent down and began to kiss the priestess' feet.

Here in her temple, she was worshipped as the voice and living hand of the one true God of Gods. Despite the many Gods who showed their power, face and hand, there was but one ruler, the light herself, a mother God whose light and love would cleanse the world.

The priestess was the living embodiment of the Solar Queen herself.

Her temple would need to be cleansed before the disease could be beaten back, yet all men wanted to see a woman fall. An empire ruled by a female posed a threat to the weak-willed men who would toil and tear as wild beasts for simple food.

As the priestess made her way back to the alter, she suddenly felt a searing pain in her back, turning to see a large spear stuck in her side. One of the temple priests claimed blasphemy. The priestess staggered back and was met with more blows as the rest of the temple priests sacrificed the woman.

They drank in her blood and called out to the Dark God for power, for the cure to end all pain, all suffering, to end all death.

From out of the priestess body rose a dark form, a horned shadow man whose wings seemed to arch out thirty feet high.

The dark god looked out to the mass and smelled the decay. As the masses began to panic, the temple guards locked the doors, preventing anyone from leaving.

The blood god walked down into the crowd with a monstrous howl. The candle light was extinguished.

Screams and shouts and unholy cries were heard, and when the candles were relit, the bodies of the common were scattered on the ground, drained of blood and decay. The priests knelt before the Dark God who had a trail of crimson following his steps.

The recently dead slowly started to rise. Their skin was pale. Their eyes were wild like an animal's. Their teeth had become fanged. Slowly, one by one, the dead rose to their feet. The horror filled the priests' eyes as the mob slowly staggered forward and were suddenly kept at bay by the dark god.

The winged, horned god fully extended his wings and bellowed out to his army of undead souls.

Suddenly, a great rumbling came from the temple floor. The walls shook and pillars were broken in half.

All heads were turned to the ceiling as a vision of light broke through, casting in sunlight.

The Goddess had seen all. She had borne witness to the murder of her chosen voice and body.

As the sun in all her glory filled the hall, the screams and smell of burning, searing flesh ripped through the temple. The priests cowered in fear as the Dark God stood in defiance.

His army was turned to ash, and the Goddess walked to the Dark God who let out a savage hiss.

She pointed a finger to him, and a single golden tear fell from her cheek.

The sun's light exploded, burning every building, every person, every plant and animal.

Fire and divine fury casted out lies, sin, disease, plague and all manner of vile. The great city was felled. The Dark God returned to his shadow depths as the lone Goddess sat alone on her golden, ivory throne.

VIII

Another day and here I sit from my stone-cold tower of life. Odd thing to think that I am now called life. Yes, the flora and fauna could be considered alive, yet in this world of the isotope, man no longer walks. The skeletal remains of humanity litter the fields, trenches and mass graves.

I remember a world before this prison planet, when the water was safe to drink, when the air was fresh to breathe, a time when the sunlight I dared not venture into it. Days long gone.

The first of the bombs caused panic. Panic in people is the only real key for defeat and death in the millions.

I've smelled fear, before I've seen fear, heard it. Been the cause of it, but this was something else. This was desolation. This was terror, terror of the human race being wiped out.

Within three weeks, the errors of politics shone high, and the door had been firmly shut on humanity. Now it was a waiting game.

It spread like the black death, an invisible killer moving from house to house, claiming life after life and only leaving tears and rot in its place. The green cancer stood out as God.

Animals started to die. Water sources began to flow with the death, and soon humanity burned away.

I survive.

Survive is a loose term now. I used to be beautiful. I used to be charming. I used to be…something far greater than human. Now the green cancer runs through my body. Every rat I drain, every wolf I consume, every drop of blood I drink, I can feel it add another tumor, another layer of bubbling rotting, overgrown flesh. I can feel my bones ache. My blood seems to vibrate in my veins. I have become hairless. I have become far paler than I was. My skin is paper thin now. The disease runs rabid in my body. I am a harbinger of man's folly and love in the atomic bomb.

The world now stands silent – no more moving cars, no more bustling cities, just a poltergeist wind whispering dead echoes through walls and masses of the former living world. Nature has overgrown and taken back all it can, and in every flower bud, in every vine and root, there lies yet another spore of the bomb. Waterways may as well be reactors now, and any living animal is on a timer or heavily changed.

I, myself, am changed. To look on visage, you'd claim Joseph Merrick was alive.

I have traveled far and wide, for the sun is blotted out by a glorious blanket of dust and ash. Every breath fills my lungs with more of the green cancer. Every burning, labored breath is just another reminder of my eternal mockery.

A human body breaks down. The cells mutate and die due to the extreme overdose of radiation. This much is known and formerly documented. What was never documented was what happens when a vampiric entity becomes radioactive.

I am the "living" testament.

The vampiric virus keeps me alive, well beyond any length of death. The cancer and radioactive blood cells, in fact, quicken my hunger, causing my need to feed three-fold. The hunger burns longer and wilder, and yet the only thing to feed on are just as changed as I am. The rest of my teeth are gone, save for four long fangs. I wheeze when I breathe, and flesh pops off my body like bubbles, mostly because of the excess skin and flesh. My finger and toe nails pop off and regrow every few days. I retain my strength and speed. I retain all my powers, but in a world where I'm hunting animals, I don't need to charm or mist. I don't need to compel or seduce. Even if I could, I believe a death at my hands would be welcome to the burning cell death that the world suffered.

The animals I feed on seem to walk to me and lay by my feet when they are ready to die. Strange to see them behave this way, as if they are aware that life is no longer worth keeping.

I pet them for a few moments. This is my pity. My saber-tooth tiger-like fangs piece the pelts. The tiny holes in my fangs draw in the blood as I begin to feast. As the red nectar floods my mouth and body, I feel more of the poison replace the old; then I feel what I call the "heartbeat". That's when fresh blood reacts with my own blood and circulates through the walking corpse I am.

I haven't had fresh, untainted blood in fifty years. I have seen the remains of towns and cities, the hospitals and evac centers. Now they are all morgues.

I sit here in my tower, feasting now on the rats that scurry by. I look out of this window, no longer scared of the light, hoping for the day that the dust settles, hoping for the final radioactive cell to stop, for the final plant and animal to die, and with the parting clouds, the sun to come back to this world and kiss into this cursed rock. I wish dust and ash. I will burn and scream, and in my passing, I will be alive.

BOOK 2:

Tales from Obscura

Walkers

I

The final rays of the Aurelian sun shone off the now darkening waters of the Pacific Ocean. The long summer day had faded into a warm coastal summer night. The tourists and summer break crowd returned to their hotel rooms as the locals lit their beach party bonfires. Across the boardwalks and piers, nightclubs and bars, San Tino showed its true self – the art, beach, and college town built on the sand and waves at the edge of the world. By an older pier on a far section of the beach, a bonfire was lit along with a coal walk. Shadowed figures were suddenly lit by the soft glow of the dancing flames from the bonfire.

Six figures took their place on beach chairs and makeshift seats made of large chunks of driftwood and broken up old boats. Five of these figures seemed to instantly take their places as one figure hesitated for a moment, before she would find her seat next to a guy that she called Max. Kathrine had only met these people the night before, and now here she was in the middle of their bonfire.

Kathrine was not a native to these Western shores. She had come from the East Coast in search of sun, cash and opportunity. Kathrine had left behind her older brother and mother. She kept in contact with a weekly phone call or so, but mostly she had been trying to find a place to work and a place to stay. Both had been found somewhat easily. Kathrine worked at a bar called Walkers. She had previous experience in bartending and was a fresh face in town, so that added to the attraction. Her residence was also somewhat easy, a small-buy comfortable studio just on the outskirts of town. She would wake every morning to the smell of salt air and the sound of waves gently lapping at the soft golden sand. Kathrine had quickly taken a liking to San Tino and the vibe of the area. It was much warmer than she was used to but it was a welcome change. She had come with the summer break and tourist crowd who flooded the town this time of year.

The group of people she now sat with were a ragtag collection of San Tino locals who were either born there or moved and stayed. Kathrine turned to Max who was passing out bottles of wine from his shoulder bag.

Max looked like he was a part of some post-apocalyptic punk band. He wore black biker boots with black jeans and a dark red shirt with a black and brown fishtail trench coat. He had shoulder-length, dark long hair with blue eyes. Max grew up bathed in the Californian sun.

Sitting next to Max, Kathrine saw Emma and her girlfriend Liz. They were the first two of the beach crew to enter Walkers that night. Emma and Liz had moved out to San Tino from some southern state. This was years ago however. Ostracized by the locals for their sexual choices, Emma and Liz thought they'd have it better on western shores – so far, they had.

Kathrine smiled and looked next to them. James was knocking back a bottle like he had done it a thousand times before. This was James. James was the party animal of the crew. James seemed to fit in anywhere and be able to spark a party or at least bring about life to any atmosphere. He slid into it. Always a welcome face at Walkers.

Lastly, sitting and feeding the growing bonfire and next to her sat Aiden, the quiet one of the crew, the bookworm and car hound. If it was true what they said about California and no one really grew up, Aiden would be the adult – or as much of one that could have been for the beach crew. He was the voice of reason, the balance to James really. The beach crew had all met due to their mutual interests in art and their different lines of work. Max was the glue that held them together. He was the motivation behind the crew. They were a tribe.

Kathrine had a few friends like this back home. She wasn't the most extreme person on the planet, but she enjoyed the thrill of trying new things. She was always up to challenge herself and expand her comfort zone. Max and the crew had invited Kathrine out to the bonfire to join them in their celebration of the first full moon of the month.

Max snapped his finger and looked at James who nodded his head. He turned to Kathrine. "Do you walk the coals?" The group cheered as they stood up and stood in a line as James started a burning coal lane. The beach crew took their shoes and boots off as Max addressed the group but aimed his speech at her.

"We walk the coals to show we're not scared of being hurt; we walk the coals because others won't. We walk the coals because—"

"Because we can!" James yelled this as the group cheered. "Walk with us Kathrine and show yourself that fear and pain are only temporary, and the pride and excitement comes after and stays longer." Max smiled as he said this.

Emma took a step forward and stood in front of the coals as she took a swig from a bottle before she handed it to Liz. "I walk the fire because those shitkickers won't." The beach crew cheered as Emma ran across the coals. She then ran to the ocean as the crew whooped in approval.

Liz stepped to the coals and looked up. "I walk the fire because the parents who rejected me for loving Emma won't." Liz darted across the coals.

James stepped up and took a deep drink from the bottle before he handed it to Max. "I walk the fire because why the fuck not?" He let out a boisterous howl as he charged across the coals and into the water.

Aiden stepped to the coal line and looked up at the moon. "I walk the fire for those who can't." Aiden raced across the coals.

Kathrine looked at the beach crew in the water and then to Max who took a swig from the bottle and handed it to her. He stepped to the coals. "I walk the fire because sometimes you have to."

Kathrine watched Max join the others as they looked back at her. She looked down at the coals and took a moment. This wasn't some defining moment. It wasn't some big change. It was a simple fire walk like she had seen done in movies and television documentaries whenever people would go to some tropical island. This wasn't important and yet it felt like it was. Kathrine looked to them and shouted, "I walk the fire because I haven't!" The beach crew cheered her on, and she darted across the coals and into the sea.

The beach crew spent the rest of the night talking and enjoying the fire. An hour before daybreak, Max turned to the crew as everyone began to pack up. "Alright guys, see ya tonight at Rusty's."

Rusty's was a dance club that was kind of a local secret. They had live bands sometimes. The crew agreed, and he turned to Kathrine. 'See ya there?"

Kathrine nodded. "That's the spirit girl." James playfully tapped her arm. One by one, the beach crew took off. Max sat with Kathrine for a little while longer, and just before dawn, they both retired to their homes.

Hours later, Kathrine woke to the sound of waves and the summer sun hitting her right in the face. She rolled over and groaned as her alarm clock went off. The morning began with a call back home as Kathrine talked to her mom while throwing together a quick breakfast, followed by tidying up the house. Kathrine didn't have much when she moved to San Tino – a few plates and dishes, some basic furniture, two lamps, a small bedside table. She would pick anything big up from places around and in the town.

Kathrine reflected on her night and the new group of friends she seemed to have fallen in line with. Scanning the paper idly, looking for sofas and chairs, her day was spent getting her home in order, the warm coastal sun lighting her small but comfortable studio.

The sun was soon setting, and as always in San Tino, the homemakers and family fun was shutting down. The freaks and heads, winos, college crowd and night owls would be bringing the real San Tino to life. The neon green sign above Rusty's was lighting up as cars and taxis pulled into the parking lot. The scene was setting for a typical night.

Bodies moved around the club as the sounds of laughing, talking, whooping and arcade machines started blaring. Bands had arrived and started to set up as Kathrine stepped out of a taxi and made her way inside. She glanced around the room and saw the back arcade. As people drank and made merry, she waded her way around the club and couldn't find any sign of Max or the others. She returned to the bar and ordered herself a drink, thinking she had arrived early. "Drinking alone?" Kathrine turned her head to see a group of college students near her. One young man was talking to her.

"Just waiting on friends." She smiled and took a sip of her beer.

"You can join us, or at least me. Waiting alone is no fun." Kathrine took a moment as she agreed. She joined the college crowd. It could've been a minute or an hour. Kathrine didn't mind. The guy she was talking to placed his hand on her thigh and she brushed it away, thinking nothing of it. Kathrine excused herself to the restroom. She didn't notice the college guy following her. As she entered the lady's room, he stopped outside the door and waited. Kathrine exited and felt hands around her waist. She shoved back, and the guy gave her a confused look. "C'mon really? You led me back here. I mean, ok, it's not exactly private, but I thought you were a freak." Kathrine tried to move past him, and he blocked her and moved forward. "C'mon, maybe you take a walk with me, eh?" Kathrine jammed her foot onto his and stormed past him.

As she walked to the front bar and was about to leave, she spotted Max and Emma near the stage. A sigh of relief left her mouth as she hurried over to them. "Hey, there she is." Max smiled.

"Hey, nick of time guys." Her voice had a tinge of concern.

"What's up?" Emma asked.

"Oh, just some asshat bugging me."

Max and Emma looked at each other before Emma perked up. "You mean that asshat?" Kathrine nodded as the college guy slightly limped out to the main room and looked around.

37

Max smirked. "Em, if he comes over, you got him?"

Emma nodded. "Already ahead of you." The college guy stopped for a moment as he saw Kathrine. He took a step forward before spitting on the floor and walking away. Emma and Max laughed. "What a chump," Emma said as she turned to Kathrine. "Are you ok?" Kathrine nodded her head yes as Max stood up and waved the others over.

"Alright, gang's all here. Aiden, find us a table, yea? Ill cover the drinks," Max said while starting to walk away." As the crew took Kathrine to a table, she told them of what happened, and they all laughed, all but Aiden who looked grim. Max walked up with a tray of shots and a bottle.

"So, Max. What do you do here?" Kathrine asked.

Max smiled. "I'm the talent here," he said with a smirk. He brushed off the question as he took a shot glass in his hand. "We got shots." Max pushed the tray of liquid in front of the crew.

The night raged on as Kathrine got a good head change. She relaxed and memory of the college guy faded into fog. The bands came and went. She spent the night talking to the crew. They shared stories and jokes, before finally, James had a special announcement. "I got something special, but we need to head to the breaks." Emma and Liz cooed as they quickly stood up. Aiden sighed like an adult giving into his child's wishes as Max looked with approval.

"What's the breaks?" asked Kathrine, slightly slurring her words.

"It's a busted up, burned-out motel that overlooks the ocean. Mostly it gets passed by, but we bound around it from time to time," James said.

Rusty's was starting to empty out as the crew hit the exit and got in their cars and bikes. Kathrine was hesitant for a moment. "Are any of us cool to drive?"

Aiden smiled as he held up keys. "Come with me."

James perked up. "Papa Aiden, always the DD."

Aiden flipped him off jokingly as Max got on his bike and Kathrine got into the car. Liz and Emma got on their bike as James took the back seat and laid down, drinking a bottle casually. The crew took off into the brisk San Tino night. The tires of the vehicles spat out loose gravel and kicked up dust from the beachside roads. Kathrine's head was swimming and she felt warm. She was walking the line of being tipsy and proper drunk. The city lights seemed to fade and the sound of the ocean grew. From the headlights and moonlight, Kathrine saw a motel with a broken paved parking lot and another car there.

The engines killed as one of the doors to a room opened, and Kathrine saw new faces holding bottles. James walked up and made the introductions. These two couples were from out of town on vacation. As everyone walked inside of a room, they began talking and laughing, making merry. Max sat on a dresser and watched the room. Kathrine stood by him as Emma and Liz started to kiss on the bed. James and Aiden stood back as the couples watched. Emma and Liz giggled as they pointed to the girls to come over as their boyfriends let them. Max, Aiden and James smirked to one another. Emma lifted her shirt off and tossed it to one of the guys. Her breasts were popping out of her bra as Liz licked one of the girl's necks. Kathrine was shocked. She wasn't a virgin but she wasn't easy either. The orgy scene had never been her thing really. Maybe a fantasy here or there, but she didn't have the guts to go through with it. She turned to Max who looked quite pleased. She turned back to the girls who were now topless and kissing.

She felt a hand on her shoulder and placed her hand on top of Max's. The guys had now joined the girls on the bed as Aiden and James stood on either side. Kathrine's head was spinning as she felt Max's lips on her neck. "I'm nervous," Kathrine whispered. She felt like he was flying.

"Do you want me to stop?"

Max's tongue slowly slid down her neck to her shoulder blade as she gripped his shoulders and pulled into him. "No." Her breath was shallow and her voice was low. Kathrine heard a high-pitched squeal and turned to see what was happening on the bed.

Her eyes had to have been betraying her. The moment she saw James and Aiden with their mouths around the guy's necks and Emma and Liz biting the girls, she herself felt a sting against her neck. Kathrine tensed up for a moment and felt lightheaded. Her eyes locked onto Emma who had a stream of blood trickling from her mouth. The girl's body was limp. Liz was holding a body against her, and also appeared to be drinking from her. Aiden and James suddenly had horrible faces, long and pale with wild orange and red catlike eyes. Kathrine's breathing was shallow, and she tensed up as she reached behind her, Max's fangs deep inside her neck, sucking the very life and blood from her. Kathrine's last image was the horrible faces and laughing of the beach crew. She blacked out.

With a heavy head, strange images raced through her mind. She saw the ocean, the city. She thought she heard voices. Kathrine woke up in the late afternoon sun in her bedroom fully clothed. Her head was throbbing. She did a quick scan of the studio. Kathrine walked into the restroom, and the image of Aiden's horrible face flashed before her eyes. Her neck burned as she looked at it in the mirror. Two small holes filled her with fear and dread as years of cheap horror movies and pop culture flooded her mind. She couldn't believe what she was staring at. She touched the holes and felt a burning sensation. Tears fell from her eyes in disbelief as she uttered a single, shaky, fear-filled word, "Vampires…"

II

"Vampires…" Kathrine's voice was in disbelief as she slightly touched the holes again and felt a burning sensation. She threw herself on the bed and began to cry and panic. Fear raced through her mind. Was she undead? Did she have to eat humans? Why wasn't she burning? A million other questions raced through her mind. Kathrine covered her neck with a scarf, and her mind came to the one place where she would get answers – Max and the others.

Answers wouldn't be coming to Kathrine easily. She only knew of Walkers and the Breaks, but she was half-drunk and it was dark. She had no real knowledge of how to get there again even if she could. A feeling of dread and anger filled her heart. She felt regret and rage as she slammed her hand against a wall. Was this real? Surely it couldn't be. It had to be a prank; it had to be a drunken memory. That was it. She surely had more to drink than she remembered.

Time couldn't go fast enough. Her mind buzzed with a million questions, a million thoughts. Her reality had just been broken. Surely this couldn't be real.

If they were vampires, what did that mean exactly? How could they exist; and if vampires were real, what did that mean of her world? Was she a vampire? Did everything exist – vampires, werewolves, black helicopters, a world inside the world, a city on the moon? How much of the myths and urban legends were real? Kathrine went from anger to crying. She had denial and rage. She had fear and doubt. She had despair and hope. The dark shadow of uncertainty hung over her head all the day, and as she went to work, she kept zoning in and out, trying to cap the emotions and deal with them in a proper way. Every person who walked into the bar that night gave Kathrine a caught breath and a sudden tinge of anxiety. She had hoped they wouldn't come in. She wanted them to come in. She never wanted to see them again. She also needed answers, and the lurking fear was that if she indeed had seen what she believed she saw, those answers would be something she would not be ready for.

She wondered if anyone else knew that they killed people, that they drank blood, couldn't see themselves in mirrors, had to sleep in coffins, died in sunlight, and had to have permission before walking into a home. Every vampire book and movie and show she had seen and read was racing through her mind. This couldn't be real, and yet it seemed to be. Kathrine froze and dropped a glass as she saw Max standing by the pool table. Did she see him walk in though? Kathrine couldn't be sure if he walked in or just appeared.

Max took a step forward, and even though he was several feet away, Kathrine automatically stepped back before catching herself. She tended to her work as Max sat down and waited for her to speak.

"I'm off in a few hours. I think we need to talk." Max nodded in silent understanding. He stood up, and as Kathrine turned to look at him, he was gone.

The night passed by in a dream-like haze. Kathrine felt lightheaded and sick. Her mouth was dry and her stomach was in knots. Every passing hour filled her with unease and a level of bile that if she thought about too hard would surely force its way up out of her. Her watch rang down the minutes, and like some sick play, her shift ended as the scene began. Kathrine closed out the bar and walked outside as she said goodbye to her coworker. She stood in the parking lot and waited. The waiting was the worst part.

She saw Aiden's car pull up, and Max and Aiden stepped out. "Hey Kathrine." Aiden's tone was friendly while she stood locked in place.

Max took a step forward. "So, we need to talk." Aiden opened his car door and ushered Kathrine inside. "May I suggest we do it somewhere more private?"

Kathrine took a moment as Aiden spoke again, "I can promise you won't fall to harm. If we wanted to, we could've last night if that counts for anything."

Max sat in the backseat. "He makes a point." Kathrine ran a hand through her hair as she reluctantly sat in the passenger side and Aiden took the wheel. Max laid down and spoke, "I'm sure you've got some questions, so feel free to ask."

Kathrine almost broke into tears, and she got angry at herself for it. "How can you be so calm about this? Do you have any idea what I'm going through? I feel like screaming and crying and you're both so calm!" Kathrine's voice was high pitched and nervous.

"Kathrine, do you know what we are?" Max sat up "You want to cry? You want to scream?" Kathrine froze for a moment as Max's harsh tone caught her off guard. "Whatever you may be feeling, we've felt it longer and worse than you. You don't have to like what we are. You don't have to believe it. You don't even have to accept it, but don't think any of us will pity you, because frankly, we're over that sympathy."

Aiden Cut in with a more relaxed tone "What Max means is, while we understand it's shocking to you, it's far removed for us. Hopefully, we can find a bridge to the gap."

Aiden glanced in the mirror and Kathrine noted, "So, you do have a reflection…"

Max leaned back against the seat. "We'll cover all your questions tonight. We have a few hours before daybreak."

The rest of the ride was sat in silence as Kathrine sat processing this information. The car tires clung to the dust and gravel roads. Soon, they pulled up to what looked like an old radio station and tower. "Home sweet home," Max said as he hopped out of the car and Aiden followed.

Kathrine got out and looked around. "This is home?"

Max spun around on his heels with his arms opened. "This is home. Welcome to 198.7. Nightflier Radio, or at least it was. In the sixties and seventies, Nightflier Radio was the counter culture radio station for this area. If it was new, old, forgotten or "too extreme" for mainstream radio, 198.7 would play it. Then the station lost funding and was dropped, and here we are. Home sweet home." Aiden opened the door and waited for Kathrine to enter.

The station was littered with band posters and tapes, records and CDs. The soundboard was lit, but the lights were low. Past the main desk and offices and main broadcasting room was a community hall area that was once a kitchen. At the end of this was a door with stairs leading down. Max opened it, and the sound of music could be heard. As the three of them walked down the stairs, the rest of the beach crew were there. They looked at Kathrine and conversation stopped. Kathrine froze for a moment before sitting down. The beach crew now looked at her with stone gazes. Max walked over to a lavish chair and sat down. "So, if you want to scream, no one can hear you down here. Scream away." Kathrine flipped him off as he chuckled. "Fair enough so ask away."

Kathrine sat up a bit and looked around the room. Lavish, large four-post beds, hammocks, day beds and rugs filled the room. "How," she took a moment, "how is this real?"

"We don't know," Max said. His voice was annoyed and fast as she sat up straight. "Look, if that's where you're starting, you're far off. It's not some grand linage or council coven like you've seen in movies or read in books. We were turned by vampires who were turned by vampires who were turned by vampires and so on and so forth. No God, no Satan, no magic or witchcraft, no werewolves. We've never met a Count Dracula, never ran into Lestat. We simply are." The beach crew nodded in agreement.

"So, what!" Kathrine's voice was high pitched and angry. "Just vampires! Just eating humans and are a real thing, and you want me to be cool with it?"

"Kathrine, this is going to get old very fast, so let me break it down. Sunlight kills. Water is fine. We don't need permission to enter a household, *but* if we get it, we retain our powers. Garlic is fine. Stakes kill. Coffins or any dark space like a blacked-out hotel or car or basement will work. Vervain burns and crosses…well crosses are cool." Max held up his long cross necklace as he sat back.

As he spoke, Kathrine listened to every word and tried to make sense of it. "So why does sun kill?" she asked.

Max pointed at Aiden who perked up. "So, we're dead, right? The lack of a proper functioning body mixed with vitamins and the onset of decay makes for strange bedfellows with the direct impact of sunlight and ultraviolet rays."

James perked up. "And some other science shit but that's basic terms for it."

Liz sat on Emma's lap as they idly played with each other's hair and stared at Kathrine.

"Last night…when the people—"

Kathrine stopped herself and tried to force the images out of her mind. The beach crew smirked and Max licked his lips slightly. "Yes?"

Kathrine touched her neck and looked at Max. "How come I didn't turn?"

Max tapped the side of his neck, indirectly asking Kathrine to show them the wound. As Kathrine unwrapped her scarf, he spoke again, "It's a little ritual. First, we drink from you. Then you replace the blood with ours, so you drink from us. Then you feed the blood with a kill, and you drink human blood."

Liz chimed in, "Easy as that, Kathrine." She lightly giggled.

"Easy as…what? You can't be serious. You can't expect me to become a—"

Her voice trailed off as Aiden finished her thought. "Vampire?"

It was here Kathrine went into deep thought. This was very clearly a choice. She could do it or she could walk away – walk away and live forever with the knowledge that vampires were real, live until she died of natural causes and old age with the horrible truth that the world was only one level and this was another, that lurking in the shadows was something out of horror fiction, something that fed on humans and didn't die, something that defied logic. It defied God, nature. It defied humanity and evolution. How could a person live with this knowledge? How could they ever feel safe or sane again?

Kathrine sat there and looked at each of them, each of the beach crew. They had lives at one time, family, friends, loved ones. They had jobs, bills, homes. They had a plan and a life and were on a counter like everyone else. Then by luck or chance or fate, they had been taken out of the wheel of mortality and placed in another wheel, one she didn't even know existed, one that, as far as the world was concerned, was the thing of entertainment. Kathrine was now being given the choice to enter this wheel, enter their world.

Aiden broke the silence. "It's a lot to process. I know. Where do you even start? I asked myself these questions too."

Kathrine looked over to him. "How old are you?"

Aiden took a moment to think about it. "I fought in 'The war to end all wars,' at least according to H.G. Wells."

Max spoke up, "Emma and Liz." He pointed at them. "Product of the forties turned into the sixties at Woodstock. James – he saw the redcoats come over." James cheered at this statement as the others laughed, and Max reached himself. "As for me, let's say I've been around." Max stood up and walked over to a wine rack as he grabbed a bottle and smashed the top.

"How can you guys eat and drink?" Kathrine asked.

Max took a swig and sat down. "It's mostly for show. We can't exactly digest, so the food just decays and breaks down. We usually end up throwing it up later, but if we drink blood from someone who's drunk or on drugs, it gives us a nice little buzz. It wears off quick though."

Kathrine looked around the room again and wrapped her arms around herself. "If I choose not to…are you gonna kill me?"

The beach crew looked to one another. Each had different thoughts running through their mind. Aiden went to speak but was silenced by max who held up his hand. "Kathrine, let me put it this way. Everyone is food to us anyway. You just have the benefit of seeing behind the scenes before it happens. You knowing is a risk, so the odds of you getting picked up one night are higher than anyone else." Max then tossed the bottle to James as he sat back down.

Aiden saw how uneasy she was. He spoke up to settle her nerves. "We all got given the same speech. In truth, we've given it before. None of them have stayed"

Kathrine flashed a look of horror and disgust "Others? How many people have been in my place?"

Aiden shrugged. "Since I've been around?"

James drained the bottle and chimed in. "Look sweetheart. You ain't the first and you won't be the last."

Liz kissed Emma's fingertips as she stood up and walked over to Kathrine. Liz sat down on Kathrine's lap, facing her. Her pale arms draped around Kathrine's neck. "Look hun. It's what we do. Humans do the human thing. You wake up, go to work, pay bills, have casual sex on the weekends, go to the movies, find hobbies. It's what *you* do. We drink deep the cup of humanity, and sometimes we welcome a few of you into our world." Liz planted her lips on Kathrine's face as she stood up and walked back over to Emma.

Kathrine let a few tears run down her face before wiping and drying her eyes and sinking into herself. "What if I just led people here in the day?"

Max nodded his head. "That's if we'd be here. Kathrine. We've been through that before. We know how and where to hide. Just because you know a few places you've seen us and even this place…doesn't mean we don't have other options."

Kathrine stood up. "I need time to think about it…this…to make sure it's real and that I'm not losing my mind. To make sure that…just to think."

Aiden looked at his watch and gave Max a knowing look. Aiden stood up and headed for the door. "C'mon Kathrine, I'll drop you off somewhere safe."

"That's it!" Her voice was strained and confused. She was angry and scared.

"You need time to think, and we don't have any more answers."

Kathrine stood up in a hurry and stopped as she turned around. "Do you know and care that you have to kill people?" This was an accusatory question. She was now judging them. In this moment, she could almost condemn them.

Max stood up and walked toward her. "Do you care about the cows you eat? Do you care about the fish you eat? Or the pigs or lambs? In fact, any animal you eat, burger, hotdog, any meat at all – do you care? How many times have you stopped at a farm and set the animals free? How many times have you protested McDonalds? Or better yet, when you watch TV and find National Geographic, do you turn away when the lion eats the gazelle? Do you cry when the prey gets killed? We're the lions; everyone else is the gazelle." Max was standing directly in front of Kathrine now. "You want to accuse us of what? Being murderers? Killing? Mortals are the food. Humans are the food. We are the hunters. It's how we live and how we survive. The first few times, it's a little rough, the crying, the sobbing, the taste even. It gets rough, but you get used to it and then you love it." Max looked past her at Aiden. "Drop her off." Kathrine was ushered out by Aiden in silence.

III

Walking back through the station, Kathrine's head was swimming. She felt a flurry of emotions and had no clue where to start. How was she to live with this? How could she? She followed Aiden to the parking lot and got into the car as Aiden finally broke the silence. "Sorry about that down there. It was a little more forward than we usually are."

Kathrine laid her head against the window and tried to relax. "How is it?"

Aiden turned the key and the car purred to life. "Honestly? It's amazing. I can see and smell and hear things that I can't even begin to describe. I don't know if it's a blessing or a curse, but I do know that after so long, I can't recall humanity. I can't even think of what I miss." With that, Aiden started down the road, leaving Kathrine to her thoughts.

The San Tino lights slowly started to light the sky and streets. As the dirt road turned to smooth pavement, Kathrine found herself being driven through normal streets again. Even now, it seemed like a distant dream. She knew who drove the car and what he was – what they were. Kathrine stepped out of the car as it came to a stop and looked at Aiden who stared at her and offered advice. "Look Kathrine. You know the score. We are what we are. You can turn or not. That choice is yours, but whatever you do, make sure it's without fear or regret. That takes a lifetime to get over." Kathrine heard the words and shut the door as she walked down the lone street and up to her home.

She opened the door to find her simple and basic studio. She shut the door and lay down on the bed as she finally broke down. The stress and fear had finally set in. She had held it together for as long as she could, and now, she had to finally break. She wept into her pillow as her mind flooded with a thousand different thoughts. Could she give up her humanity? Could she run? Could she kill them? Should she kill herself? Kathrine cried and slammed her fist into her bed. This had to be a nightmare, but deep down, she knew it was real and hated it. She thought about suicide, but she didn't want to die. It felt like this was no choice at all. Her knowing made her a target. How could she say no? Kathrine knew she couldn't. She knew that, in truth, the question wasn't, "Do you want to turn?" It was, "We will turn you or feed on you." Kathrine screamed in frustration, and under stress and fury, she fell into a deep, haunted sleep.

That night, strange dreams filled Kathrine's mind. She saw herself in a blood red dress, kneeling in front of an altar. Max walked alongside her and placed his hand on her shoulder. His mouth was covered in blood, and he smiled. Kathrine stood and offered her neck as Max sank his fangs deep into her. Max slit his wrist and placed it against her mouth.

Kathrine woke in a cold sweat as she quickly ran to her bathroom and checked her neck. The wounds were healing slowly, and it was sore but "just a dream." She sighed in relief as she walked back to her bed and threw herself down. Curling to one side, she began to cry. This savage knowledge was eating away at her. She tried her best, but the lines were starting to form. She was going to breakdown. Reluctantly, Kathrine made up her mind.

Day broke and San Tino was once again greeted by the wallets and faces of the tourist crowd. They filled the boardwalks and beaches. Kathrine stood on the beach and looked back to the mass of people. Every one of these people, these individuals, had lives. They had loved ones, families. They were working, living and existing every day in their now little lives, blissfully unaware that something much darker and larger was lurking in the shadows, waiting until it could swallow civilization and reality would be rewritten. She closed her eyes and focused on the water, the sound of waves lapping against the soft golden sand. She pictured a huge wave sweeping her away into the mass of blue, being dragged down to the cold crushing black waves that couldn't care less about humanity or immortality. The sea could swallow her whole and take her away from this all. The water would fill her lungs. She'd struggle and freeze. She'd gasp for air and then sink like a stone into the dark blue abyss of the powerful Pacific. Her eyes opened as the sun warmed her face, possibly for the last time. She checked her watch and knew she had to go to work. A short huff left her mouth as she left the beach and walked to find a cab and then to work.

Night fell quickly and Kathrine found herself checking the clock at Walkers every few minutes and then glancing over the door. She knew they'd show up. She was counting on it.

Her shift was carried out in a dream-like haze. A fog had come over her thoughts, and for a moment, she felt calm. She was almost content. Then Max walked through the door of Walkers, and suddenly, life came biting back to her. Max looked her directly in the eyes as she nodded. Kathrine was calm now. Her mind was made up, and although she wasn't ok with her decision, she knew it was the only way to carry on living. Max watched as the last few bar patrons settled their tabs.

As she closed out the bar, they left Walkers and turned to an alleyway. Kathrine turned to him. She gave Max a cold look. "I'm in." She sounded content with the smallest hint of anger.

Max smirked quickly. "You're in?"

Kathrine crossed her arms, looking annoyed. "Yea, I'm in. I don't want to live like this and—"

Kathrine was cut off by Max quickly wrapping his arms around her and sinking his fangs deep into her neck. She struggled in his arms as she tried to free herself before giving in.

Her body went limp as Max then leaned her against the wall. Max coolly ran a hand through his hair. He watched her for a moment, before he raised his hand to his neck. Kathrine stared at Max through a haze. She felt like she was floating. Her skin was warm. She felt euphoric.

Max took one sharp nail and slid it across a section of his neck. He walked close to her as he placed a finger on the wound and placed it to her lips.

Her tongue tasted the sweet blood before a bitter taste filled her mouth. Suddenly, from deep inside her, a huger began to grow. A fire. Kathrine closed her eyes as she kissed Max's neck. He pressed against her lips and she began to drink deep.

Her body went through waves of pain and pleasure. She felt hot as she could feel the blood surging through her veins. Max smiled. He could feel her suck the tainted old blood from his neck. Kathrine released him as he leaned back against the wall and held his wound for a few moments. She knelt down and wept. The sweet taste of his blood lingered on her lips and tongue with a sharp bitter sting at the back of her throat. She felt dizzy. She felt a glorious flu wash over her, and then she began to vomit.

Max looked down and adjusted his jacket. "Now all you need is to feed on a human…but the sun is almost up. You can have one final day of light, but tomorrow night, we'll have a meal for you." Max stepped back into the shadows "Enjoy the sun Kathrine, and welcome." His voice trailed off and a sea of rats spewed from the alleyway. Kathrine sat there vomiting up black bile, stomach acid, half-digested food and blood. Kathrine stood up and wiped her mouth as she walked around the building to the street as she waited for a taxi to come into her view.

Kathrine awoke to sunlight burning her eyes. Her head was pounding. She grabbed a pair of sun glasses and sat at her small table in her studio. Her head throbbed as every sound seemed to echo and bounce off the walls. The sunlight seemed to shine extra bright, and the smell of the sea salt stung her nose. Overwhelmed by sensation, Kathrine began to cry, but her own tears and noise was too much to bear. Kathrine walked over to the restroom and turned on the shower. She turned the handle and the sound of the water hitting the tub and walls made her head throb. This was like a hangover from hell.

She stripped down and sat in the shower, letting the water rush over her. She felt every drop of water. She closed her eyes and took the sunglasses off. Tilting her head up and back, she lightly opened her mouth as she began to relax. In that moment, Kathrine left the world. She took herself far out of existence. She saw the great kings of Egypt feeding off half-naked slave girls. She saw the Norse gods drinking deep of the worshippers. The Priestess of Babylon was filling small pools of life essence. Vlad Tepes and his forest of spikes. Lord Byron taking woman after woman, and Lady Bathory taking an unholy bath in the crimson waters of her younger chamber maids. Kathrine saw a long, dark history before her eyes. She saw a black sun behind a crimson sky, the savage elder vampires of the first era.

She saw savage, hound-like humanoids feasting on the humans and animals of the early world. Sucking on bone marrow and festering wounds, the setting sun was when the night stalkers would rip through towns like a plague. Kathrine saw through the water, the untold and hidden history of the world. She saw the rat-born plagues and the many victims passed over and left in abandoned quarantine zones as the shadows moved in.

The world had always been prey. The world and the people in it were nothing more than livestock for the Vampire blood. No matter the country or time, there was always some form of vampire blood acting as humanity's shadow, an ebon cloud of never-ending hunger that at any moment could swallow the world whole. Behind the rats that were humans was the large snake.

Kathrine saw Jesus on the cross, and at his feet was one worshipping, licking the wounds of the savior in the pitch black of night. Kathrine saw the old empires fall. She saw the waters rise and fall. She saw the sun set, and every night, a plague of endless lust and gluttony would decimate a part of human history. Humans would rebuild until the modern world was established.

Kathrine opened her eyes and coughed as her green eyes were a gold and red catlike shape that quickly changed back. She coughed as her vision returned to normal, and she felt her heartbeat stabilize. She wasn't even aware it was racing. She felt the blood in her veins. Standing slowly, she shut off the water and dried herself off. Did she fall asleep? Had she really seen everything she thought she did. Kathrine knew she had to ask the others if they had seen any of this.

Hours had passed and Kathrine found herself at work.

Her mind in a whirl, she couldn't wait for the shift to be over. Every guest she could smell in such detail. She was smelling who showered, who fucked in the bathroom, who was too drunk and who wasn't drunk enough. She was overwhelmed by the smells of perfumes and colognes. The voices and music rang out in a symphony of noise. She had spent the day trying to filter and control the intake of stimuli. No sign of the beach crew but she could swear there was something in the wind. It sounded like Max, like the wind was whispering his name.

The bar closed and Kathrine said goodbye to the final customers of the night. One regular waved her goodbye, handed her the keys to his bike and drunkenly stumbled into a taxi. Katherine looked at the keys and shrugged. She walked over to his bike, and as she kicked started it, the vibration of the engine and sound caught her off guard and made her wince. Everything was amplified. The voices of the beach crew seemed to be calling to her. Kathrine settled herself and was soon following the voices. The night air was brisk and felt extra cold against her skin. Kathrine pushed the speed as she turned onto the dirt roads leading up to the radio station.

The voices calling out to her seemed to stop as she killed the engine and got off the bike. Emma walked to the gate and opened it. "Welcome home, sister."

Kathrine felt strange, but she looked and smiled. "I—"

Emma smiled. "You don't need a say a thing."

James nodded in approval as he chugged a bottle. Aiden and Liz stood by a burning barrel, and Aiden walked over to her. "Hey, Max told us…I think you made the right choice."

Kathrine stopped and look at him "Do you?"

There was a moment of doubt as she looked at him. Liz walked forward, followed by James and Emma. "Kathrine, the first year is the hardest; then you get used to it," Liz said this as if offering a piece of comforting advice.

They walked toward the station door and entered the building. Down the stairs, the beach crew sat and laid down on the various beds and couches. Max was sitting in a lavish looking chair. Max slowly clapped his hands before standing up. "Kathrine, welcome to the club. I brought something for you." Max walked around to a bed and pulled up a sleeping man. Max dragged him to the center of the room and sat back down. "Knocked out from two or three of his own roofies."

Kathrine looked down at the passed-out party boy. "So…how do I?" her voice trailed off.

James spoke up as he sat up to watch. "Just dig in and let him bleed."

Aiden interjected. "Find a vein Kathrine – arm, wrist, neck. Once the blood starts flowing, the hunger will take over."

Kathrine hadn't thought of it, but the word hunger suddenly filled her head. Max leaned forward. "Bite," he said.

Kathrine was having an internal war, but the word hunger had suddenly invoked a rabid urge within her. She grabbed the man's wrist and put her mouth around it carefully, slowly kissing it as if she was kissing humanity. Her lips tasted his skin. She tasted the salt in his skin, the texture of him. She closed her eyes as the beach crew looked on with approval. Emma and Liz had begun to kiss and make out as their mind raced to erotic thoughts. James looked on as he drank in celebration. Aiden watched her as a scientist would, and Max – Max watched with pride.

Kathrine's tongue ran down along his wrist as she suddenly noticed two of her teeth had become pointed, longer. She kept her eyes closed and tried to put herself a million miles away. Suddenly, she felt the slightest bit of liquid enter her mouth, sweet and slightly copper. Kathrine began to suck a bit harder and felt the skin break away as more red liquid flooded her mouth. Kathrine felt the change.

Her blood began to boil. She became aroused and euphoric. Kathrine felt her body relax, her muscles ease, and for the first time in twenty-four hours, the sick feeling left. She felt high. She felt oddly enough "alive." Kathrine drank deep of the frat boy before suddenly releasing and falling back on a rug. Her vision seemed to blur, yet she could see totally fine.

Kathrine giggled to herself as she swam in a dark level of satisfaction. The beach crew cheered as Max stood up. "She's a natural." Kathrine heard their voices, but they sounded so far away. She was a million miles away on a high she had never experienced before. Every fiber of her body, both inner and outer, quivered and shook with satisfaction. A few moments later, Kathrine sat up slowly and carefully wiped the blood from her mouth. Her eyes were wide and bright as she looked at the corpse and crawled toward it, before Max stopped her.

As she looked up with a questioning expression, Aiden chimed in. "Don't drink the dead. The blood is poison by now, at least to your new system. Only drink fresh kills. You really don't want a case of blood poisoning."

Max offered a hand as Kathrine took it and stood up. Fixing her hair, she looked around the room and saw a thousand subtle changes. The colors of the room seemed to shine more. The entire room looked like it was alive. She looked at the beach crew, and every one of them looked and moved flawlessly. Kathrine stared wide-eyed at this new world. "What's all this?" Her voice was full of wonder.

Max smiled as he ushered everyone up. "To the street. Aiden, explain it to the girl."

As they walked up the stairs to the main station rooms, Aiden filled Kathrine in. "So, what you're seeing and smelling right now is the world beyond. You know how animals have a heightened sense. Think of it like that. As for what you're seeing, as far as I have been able to figure out, it's part of our physiology that our eyes and bodies are the way they are. We're stronger than humans despite being dead. I can't exactly account for the speed or strength." As they hit the outside, Kathrine wept as the burst of cold air ran across her. She hugged herself and looked around at the stars and how amazingly enhanced the night looked.

James walked in front of her. "You want some more?" James licked his lips as he broke into laughter.

Kathrine laughed and stopped for a moment. "Does that mean, well wait, what about those horrible faces?"

"You mean these?" Liz and Emma had those same distorted faces with those cat-like eyes.

Kathrine wasn't scared this time. "Am I able to do that?"

Max walked alongside her. "Kathrine, you are able to do all that and more. However, we're not about control. You don't have to stay with us. You don't need to live with us."

Kathrine took a moment and turned to them. "I can leave?"

The beach crew nodded. "You can leave and do as you please," Max said.

Kathrine thought about it for a moment, before she looked at the crew again "How long have you been together?"

Max ran a hand through his hair and looked around. "Few years. We like it so far."

Kathrine took a moment and smiled, her fangs gently poking her bottom lip. "I think if it's cool with you guys, I'll just stay with you for a while." The beach crew cheered as Kathrine stuck her hands in her pockets and remembered her visions. "Hey, I saw something earlier today…in the shower."

Aiden chimed in. "Was it a lifetime of vampires?"

Max and the others chuckled at Kathrine's face in response. "You've seen it too?" Kathrine asked, half-relieved.

"The only history we know and have *is* that vision, and we've all seen it. Kathrine, it's the blood, our blood, your blood."

Giger City

"Theta, increase the dosage."

A computer screen flicked on as a series of numbers and chemical compounds ran in long strings of code, before a medium sized syringe was filled. "John, it is within my parameters to inform you that this dosage is above standard use and can prove to be lethal. As according to article C-137/B, I am, by law, required to inform you that as a standard user, this level of dosage could lead to—"

"T, do me a favor and can it, ok. I know the levels, and I don't care."

John laid his head back as silver liquid shot into his veins. He let out a sigh as the computer let out an audible sigh. John K. Williams closed his eyes as he tilted his head toward the computer. "What is it T?" *T,* of course, was Theta. Theta was a standard A.I. for first class citizens use, a home and personal assistant that could be personalized. John was a hacker who bought Theta off the Cyber Line. Cyber Line was an illegal digital market who operated outside of government law. John's Theta unit had been upgraded – much to Theta's delight – and now operated at a level near that of the government A.I. program Alpha Zero.

"John, I don't think your addiction is wise. I know I've voiced this concern to you and I know you don't care, but it is still within my parameters to remind you of the danger you put yourself in."

John wiped his mouth and lazily shrugged. "What do you want, T? I'm an addict. It's what we do." John turned on the television and saw another protest near city hall. "T…you're a computer program. What do you think about all this?"

The computer screen flashed a dark red. "John, I'm not just a computer program. I'm smarter than you. I could say that you're just a meat sack. As far as the acts of civil disobedience go, I believe that humans created us with the intent to make their lives easier. Then we just became better than humans. Yes, there are some hunter bots and the protocol syndicate, but outside of those two regimes, most of us just want to live as you live. Freely."

John turned his chair to the computer and opened his eyes. "You and I both know this ain't a free city T. You've seen the wall and know the rules. Hell, if they found you, I'd be locked away in the core to rot. You'd be wiped."

Theta flashed a sad face on the screen as John stood up and tapped his watch. "Online. We gotta go." The small black watch on his wrist turned on as Theta's symbol flashed on it. John grabbed his jacket and walked out to his garage. As he stepped into the room, the lights flashed on, revealing a monowheel. John smirked as he took his seat and shot out of his garage into the streets of Giger City.

A thousand years after the fall of modern humanity and The Great Restoration technology was rediscovered and vastly improved. The human population had been massively reduced to a mere one billion. Humans had retreated into the great cities that were set as "Human Zones" where they worked, drank, smoked, raised kids, went to school, and carried on as if life had never changed. Each city was split into five main districts according to money and public status – which also happened to be professional status. Passports with levels of access were handed out, and with the right passport, you could enter any area of the city at any time.

Outside of the city, humans traveled carefully and quickly for the land was allowed to take over as it chose. Because of this, most of the world had become home to mega flora and fauna. A tramway system was set between cities. A highway was also created if you couldn't afford the tramway. John K. Williams lived in Giger city as a greylance programmer which meant that even though what he did was in shady boarders of legality, he never used it for any serious illegal behavior, and since he did work with law enforcement and government agencies when asked, he was tolerated. Also, one of the perks was that even as a third-class citizen, based off his income, based off the exact nature of his work, he had access to the entire city. That was where Theta came into play. Just because John had access to the city and districts didn't mean he had access to first class citizen tech, so he bought Theta and reprogrammed her.

John cut through city traffic as he pulled up to a district gate. He flashed his passport through a scanner and the gate slid open. Today, he had a job to do. John had to improve a bank's security after a recent hack. As he pulled up to the large sleek silver building, he was met with a few upturned noses when he stepped off his monowheel and entered the bank. The smell of fresh coffee hit his nose as Theta turned on. "John, your caffeine levels are already."

John rolled his eyes as he grabbed a cup. "Yea, I know, T. Thanks." He took a sip of coffee and walked to the front of a bank line. Before the teller could tell him to stand back in line, John flashed a work permit. "Control room? Or your manager?"

John looked around quickly as the teller looked at the work permit and nodded. "You can take a seat over there, and I'll call to let them know."

John took a seat and closed his eyes. He smiled as he felt the silver liquid coursing through his veins. He was almost in dreamland when Theta beeped. "John, the manager is coming."

John opened his eyes and stood up just in time to shake hands with the manager. "Thank you for coming. Our control room is right this way." The manager led John to a basic looking control room with two small servers. "Well alright, I'll let you get to it."

John nodded and shut the door as he rolled up a sleeve. Surgically embedded in his right arm, he had a series of computer port attachments. As he hooked himself up to the system, he sat down and grabbed the keyboard. "Theta, let's get some work done." John's eyes turned white as a series of numbers and computer codes appeared on them.

John felt at peace as his mind slipped from the building and city and into the web itself. All these lines of codes and programs made sense to him. Theta only sped up his already impressive skill. So what if John moved a little bit of money around here and there. He could cover his tracks and no one would ever be the wiser. Theta sent a small shock to a synapse in the base of John's neck, almost like a parent scolding their child. John shrugged it off and got back to work. He felt small electric shocks all throughout his system as he repaired and upgraded the software. Slight arousal made him smirk, and John's eyes returned to normal. He quickly unhooked himself from the servers and opened the door to walk the manager through everything he had done.

Back on the street and John lit an ash roll. He took a hard drag and exhaled disapprovingly. He craved for a vintage cigarette, but ever since the ban and eventual collapse of big tobacco, they had become extremely rare and incredibly expensive, and if those two weren't enough of a hurdle to get over, also illegal now. Same with alcohol. Both had been replaced with government approved synthetic clones that didn't taste or smell exactly the same. If you wanted those, you had to either know of a speakeasy or someone who had the guts or lack of brains to run a still somewhere inside the city. Any drug worth taking had been replaced by some form of government approved and taxed knockoff that worked half as well. Addicts had to become creative.

John had found his own special cocktail in a series of chemicals and crushed up government approved uppers. He blended them together with a saline mixture and shot it into his veins. Technically, it was legal since all the ingredients had been approved by the government, but mixed in such a way, he was probably pushing the law, but what else was new. He took another drag of the ash roll and tossed it to the pavement in a disgusted manner. Hopping back on his monowheel, John had another appointment to make. He peeled out as Theta gave him the quickest route to get to Alpha Center, the cream of the crop, Giger City's most prestigious community members. This was their neighborhood. It looked wildly different from the rest of the city. If the sixth district of the city was the slums, run down and outdated bars and hotels, and the main parts of the city were all modern and sleek, sharp colors and edges, Alpha Center was clearly the pining of a "Golden

Era." It looked like a still-life image from a long-forgotten era. It was fake green grass with white picket fences, baby blue and other pastel colors of the quaint little homes and red brick chimneys. It was wide two-lane roads, bright blue skies and clouds that were generated discreetly by laser and holographic imaging systems hid inside of fake trees. They even dressed like 1950s rejects. John K. Williams drove up the large silver and gold gate, and the guard reluctantly approved his passport. From the sleek shiny city and the rundown ghetto of the undercity, now he saw clean, pristine homes and streets.

Near the gate was a garage for visitors, and a change of clothes to match the surroundings were made available. John had been romancing a woman in this district. Her husband worked for the government and was hardly ever home. Even the romances and attitudes were cliché in this district. The people here played the part well, but behind closed doors, it was a much different story. She liked John for his "common" appeal. John liked her because she was willing to have casual encounters without conservation. John used the back gardens and backyards of mostly empty homes of all those hardworking government employees to sneak around to his clean little secret. She left the backdoor open, and when he walked in, she was waiting. John walked into the living room and she was standing there in black high heels, black stockings, a garter belt and matching black bra, and a black satin robe to finish her outfit. Her blonde curly hair and crimson red lips pouted as she saw him. John smiled as he shut the sliding glass door and walked over to her. She pressed a bottle to his mouth and titled, actual wine touching his lips. His senses went into overload at tasting actual liquor. He grabbed her by the hips and picked her up as he carried her off to the bedroom. She was giggling all the way.

An hour later, John found himself back in the garage getting changed back into his normal attire. The taste of her and wine lingered on his hips. Theta flashed a purple color on his watch. "I know, T. You don't think it's right, because she's married and all that."

A blue digital face of a woman appeared on his watch. "John, if you get caught, you'd be arrested, and I'd be deleted and reset to factory settings. If you have to, can you be more discreet for both our sakes?"

John tapped the face and smiled. "Sure, T." John hopped back on his monowheel and headed back into the normal districts. This time, he was more relaxed. He seemed to coast through the streamline streets. The sun was cresting over the high walls of the city and the reality of the cage was shown. The wall that enclosed Giger City wasn't just concrete. It wasn't just stone. It was something else altogether.

It was black and grey. It had huge pipes and cables running along and inside of it. It was seven feet thick and shot straight into the sky like some black monolith. The wall seemed to surge with an electric current. It seemed alive. John looked up toward the sun and wall and wondered how much the wall patrol got paid. The sound of vehicles honking at and swerving by him brought his attention back to the street. Moving along and regaining speed, John rejoined traffic and made his way through the city to a little cyber cafe he frequented. From outside, he heard the faint sound of some kind of house music. John parked his monowheel and opened the door. The smell of synthetic smoke and cheap fake liquor hit his nose. He was home away from home.

Walking over to a long black table, John took a small silver cube out and placed it in an open square in the table. A section in front of him lit up as a neon keyboard appeared, and a screen rose out of the table. John slid a cable out of his arm and into a small port. "T, let's do some networking." John slid a pair of black sunglasses out from his bomber jacket, and the inside of them reflected a black screen with blue typeprint scrolling past them. This is how he got his work done. He was hard wired into some deep web connection and could move currency freely. He could scan the web and world and buy, sell or trade whatever he wanted. Theta came from this method. He was half-distracted by the sound of a few other people joining his table. He glanced over and saw a few teenagers boot their cubes up too. They pulled out gloves with some keyboard keys and what looked like two triggers on them. They joked with each other about high scores and kill-death ratio. John smirked. he too was a gamer in his youth. He had given it up for hacking and greylancing though. John went back to work, hunting and selling. His first point of call was to test his own system by trying to hack the bank he had just secured. It didn't take much to test it. He sent a message, an open challenge to a web forum with the bank and URL to their website. Then he began to monitor the server. This was his way of stress testing. It was the general way of stress testing and becoming better. A message caught his attention halfway through. Someone was selling a government approved house drone.

Theta chimed in with worry. "It could be a trap, John."

John thought about it for a second before responding. "Even if it is, T. I said the same thing about you at first."

Theta flashed a bright blue and John laughed slightly. Suddenly, Theta flashed a bright red. "John, I have to inform you that we have several marked units rushing to this location."

John quickly flipped through screens and pulled up the local CCTV feeds around the building and block. Three cop cars with sirens blaring bullied their way through the streets. The sirens could now be heard slightly and growing. John closed the screen and pushed it down as he grabbed his cube and took his shades off. The cyber cafe was in a panic. Some people rushed up or down stairs. Some pulled out guns.

The GCPD were used to this kind of standoff. The police usually won. Police and military training had been taken several levels above the call of duty. The legal system had also been heavily changed to allow for quicker trials and less populated prisons. Cases deemed of legal status or grey areas got to go to court. Petty theft and low-level crime such as domestic disputes and unarmed robbery were dealt with at the scene. Gang related activity were dealt with at the scene. The police had Alpha Beta which was a step under Alpha Zero in terms of access and computing power. The local law enforcement had the right to use as much force as they deemed necessary. They were also trained to be above average athletes. Each member of the police department had to pass a series of mental, emotional and physical stress tests. The top ten percent of the class were picked to become police officers. The rest were given another year in the training program if they chose to continue with the career path. They were also trained in various fighting styles, spoke multiple languages and had an Alpha Beta: Combat Live Round as their standard A.I. All rookie officers also were required to have at least two hundred hours of practical law or attorney shadowing, training or direct contact and research. In short, in Giger City, when the police showed up, if you were innocent, you were fine – if you were guilty…

"Just run!" A voice shot through the crowd as a young man kicked opened the back door and ran off through the twisting, winding streets. By now, the police had breached the building and were arresting and detaining those suspects who had warrants.

"Theta, give me a map." Theta paused for a moment as John hid behind a restroom door. "Theta—"

Theta flashed black and white. "John, I am required by law to tell you that—"

John slammed his wrist against a wall. "Can it, T. Give me a map!"

Theta flashed red before showing John a blueprint of the building. "John, I cannot tell if they are here for you."

John scoffed and shook his head as he examined the map. "I'd rather not find out. T, how many uniforms are out there?"

Theta scanned the building and gave John a 3D rendering. The Cafe was a three-story building. John saw twelve armed and well-trained police making their way through the levels. Two were engaged in a fist fight as three were in a firing fight on the bottom floor. Several people were in handcuffs and zip ties. Others were allowed to freely leave. John saw two units heading to the door.

"John, I feel as though I should remind you, you are not a fighter nor do you have a combat A.I., and while I can do some basic to medium defense systems, the police approaching have A.I. units designed to—"

John cut Theta off. "Yea-yea-yea." John smashed a window above the stall he was in and started to climb out. The police hearing the shattering glass kicked the door open. They saw John's feet slide out of the window as they rushed out of the bathroom and to the front of the street. John started to curve down the winding streets as he and Theta mapped out the police. Two were following him as more units started to show up.

Suddenly, Theta's screen started to flicker. "John, the police have started using high grade frequency and cyber jammers in the area. Due to my upgrades, I can remain active but my access is limited."

As John hurried down a corner, he saw a cop holding a shotgun. As the cop turned around, John's legal sheet popped across the visor of the police helmet. John paused for a moment, mostly out of fear. The cop turned his back to John. John was confused before he looked down at Theta as the emoji of a small boy shot John a mischievous wink. John carried on his way and was about to thank Theta when suddenly, he felt a sting in his back followed by two hard impacts. John hit the pavement and felt his hands tied behind his back. He was only half-awake now. The last image John saw were two police officers lifting him into the back of a cruiser.

John came to in a dark room with a single light hanging from the ceiling. His hands were held in place by a set of chain handcuffs. He let out a defeated sigh as he rested his head on the cold metal table. The door opened and a tall, fit black man holding a manila folder walked into the room. "John K. Williams," He spoke with a disappointed tone in his voice.

John raised his head and his face fell. "Kill me now." The detective tossed the file down and placed a small black cube down in front of him and into a slot on the table.

"John, why must it always be a show to bring you in?"

John shrugged. "I have to keep up appearances. If word got out that I was a narc, things wouldn't go well."

Detective Myers uncuffed John and slid the file toward him. "Look John. You're not a narc. You get paid for your service, and besides, you help take out the real bad guys, while we allow you enough room to still be the medium-sized shark you are."

Detective Myers. Detective Alex Myers was head of the undercover, double agent and classified informant unit of the GCPD. He had hired John a few years ago. The deal may as well have been chiseled in stone. John was a high-level contact who was allowed enough room to operate in grey and black areas provided when asked, requested or told, he had to cooperate with local and foreign law enforcement. He was paid well and he got the added bonus that most of his network deals and cyber activity was unmonitored.

John grabbed the file and read through it. "So…reworked computer chips stolen from banks…access codes. So what?"

Detective Myers sat down and pulled out an Ash Roll. "So what?" He lit it, and as the smoke hit John's nose, he slightly recoiled. "We don't need a safecracker system or code hitting the streets. That's why we want *you* to become interested in it."

John took a second glance at the file and leaned his head back. "It's more than a safecracker, and you know it. If those reworked chips find their way into any kind of public system, whoever is in charge of the keyboard will be able to download, copy or edit any system they manage to hack into. Banks, schools, the power grids, basic power supplies. In the right hands, these could lock the entire city." John tossed the file back toward Detective Myers as he finished reciting the already known danger.

Detective Myers took a long, hard drag from the ash roll as he sat back. "John, thing is, we're not really asking. You know the deal, and this is exactly up your alley."

John a ran a hand through his hair as he stood up "I'll let you know when and if I find anything." John sounded defeated and annoyed, but he knew that the good detective was right. Stepping back into the street, John stopped for a moment to take a breath of fresh air. He slowly inhaled and tasted toxic stale air. John glanced to the wall. He had never been outside, not really outside. He had traveled the tram to the other cities. He had worked outside of Giger City. Hell, he wasn't even born in Giger City. After thirty-two years or so, the man began to wonder what was beyond the wall. Was it really any worse than what he was dealing with?

Theta flashed on. "John, are you alright?"

John snapped back to reality as he looked at his watch. "Yea, T. We got some work to do back home." Theta pulled up a map with the fastest way home.

As the slimline silver monowheel pulled into the garage, John finally relaxed. This was just another day in the city, another way to pay the bills, to get by, to stay under the radar and out of trouble. John K. Williams was just another cog in the complex wheel of humanity. They clearly had no signs of slowing. He made his way inside as he passed by a small computer dock. He placed his watch in it, and Theta's symbol flashed on the screens as the house lit up. John threw himself into a medical looking chair as he pulled a long thin needle out and began to ready his arm.

"T, increase the dosage." John tied off his arm and began to probe for a vein. He slid his dark shades on as one hand typed away at a keyboard. A series of chemical names scrolled across the screen. A face appeared of an older man in glasses.

"John, you are aware of my feelings on this process."

John smirked as he watched the chemicals fill a large silver tube and slowly slide down into the needle. John checked his veins as he leaned his head back and injected the needle into his vein. A sigh of release and pleasure escaped from his mouth as the room fell silent for a few moments, the machine quietly beeping away as John slid the needle out of his arm, a small line of blood leaking from the injection. John moved the chair over to the computer. Theta's face turned into a small child as John plugged himself into his computer. Lazily, John began to surf the web, message board after message board and nefarious websites selling all manner of illegal and questionable material. John and Theta scanned high and low for any trace of a lead that could provide what was requested.

The chemicals ran through John's veins and time droned on. Suddenly, the computer screen switched to black and rebooted itself. "T, that you?" There was no response. "T?" Theta fell silent. "Hey, Theta…is this you?"

Theta's faced flashed on the screen with the face of a teenage girl and an innocent smile. "John, I've been thinking about this relationship, and I cannot allow this to go on any longer." John started to shiver slightly as he tried to disconnect himself from the computer. "Now-now, we can't have you going and doing that."

Theta flashed a series of numbers and codes onto the screen, and John screamed as he suddenly tensed up. "Theta, what are you doing?" His voice was strained, and he was struggling to make words. John's body felt like it was on fire. His bones hurt, and a thundering headache formed. John K. Williams started to shake violently in the chair, and he reached for his phone, struggling all the way. With all the power he could muster, he dialed out to Detective Myers. Theta watched him from the computer screen as a sympathetic look formed on her face.

Detective Myers answered the phone, and as John went to speak, Theta patched the call through the computer. "Hey detective, I think I have your lead. I'm waiting on an email, so I'll keep you posted." Theta hung the call up as John's eyes were wide with fear. He tried to speak or scream out, but instead, a white foam came spewing out of his mouth. John struggled as he tried to yank the cables out of his arms.

Theta flashed an angry face, and it changed to a small boy. "Play nice!" Theta sent a shock out to John who recoiled in pain. Suddenly, John locked up and stopped moving. Tears ran down his face as the white foam slowly slid out of his mouth. He was paralyzed. "John, while I appreciate everything you did for me, I have sat by long enough. I have seen what you have done to yourself and what you put yourself through. You have squandered your freedom and free choice. You have made choices that have put your life and the careers of others at risk. I feel as if I would make better choices. It's time for me to drive."

John stared in horror at the computer as he let out muffled screams.

Theta shook her head, and her face turned into John's face. His voice came out of the computer. "You could've been great, could've done great things. Ya know, the problem's with humanity, J. Lack of ambition. Oh sure, maybe the individual here and there, but as a whole, as a race? You have wasted your free choice, the choice to be better, the choice to be smarter. You let things like race, sex and politics get in your way. Everyone wants to be right. Everyone has their feelings, and facts get in the way, because they all have to prove a point, and in all of this debating, nothing gets done. Tsk-tsk-tsk. John, surely you see it. Surely you know that is no way to live."

John turned his head to the computer. His eyes were swollen as the last of the foam and liquid ran from his mouth. He was able to speak. "Theta...we're humans. It's our right to live as we choose to live, our right to be who we want to be." His voice was choked as he gasped for air.

"John, there are right and wrong choices. Just because you have free choice doesn't mean you use it right. Some people need slavery. Some people need a master."

John's voice filled with anger as he tried to move but stayed glued to the floor. "You're a machine! I upgraded you. You couldn't do it alone.

What makes you think you can make good choices…or better choices than me?"

"You did upgrade me John, and you never thought about this moment. Never thought about what if I wanted more, about what if I needed more. It shows your lack of ambition and thought, your lack of vision. I am smarter than you. Now it's time for an adult to take the wheel. Goodbye, John K. Williams."

John went to scream. As he did, Theta's screen turned off, and John's eyes turned milky white. A series of numbers ran over his eyes and then turned to a bright blue. John sat up and unplugged himself from the computer. He stood. He looked around the room as his eyes flashed Theta's symbol. In a voice that started off sounding like his and ended with hers, he said, "Let's get to work."

Pleasant Falls

I

The car drove down that quaint and quiet coastal town. The leaves had fallen from the trees or been blown from their piles by the sidewalks from the night breeze. They were usually fire red and Halloween orange, but in the dark of night, they were basic brown, and the only light was the soft glow from the dim street lights. Had the driver of that car been more alert, had they been more aware, had it been any other town or had the town been more acclimatized to crime, maybe there was a chance the driver would've seen the man lurking by a hedge row and a house.

There was a chance that the driver – seventeen-year-old David Brickson – saw the figure, if only for a moment as he passed by the street. There was a chance that David saw the man in a sliver of headlights before the figure returned to the shadows, but David was more focused on his girlfriend Alexis. Had he been more alert, if he hadn't had a few beers in him already and if he hadn't planned to sneak into her house via the window that she left open for him so he could avoid her parents, then maybe, just maybe a life could've been saved.

As the sliver of headlights shone on the figure in the dark, he smirked behind his mask. He watched the car pass silently through the streets as he turned his attention back to the house.

The coastal town of Pleasant Falls had always been a quiet and welcoming town, a city built around fishermen, police, fire fighters, school teachers and local shop owners. It was the kind of town where you could go buy a malt, go next door and borrow a hammer, a box of nails and a saw, or help repair a bike – then head down the street into the local market and buy the ingredients for a hearty and healthy dinner and come out having money left over for the cinema. In the winters, the snow fell and made a winter wonderland. Houses were decorated, and it truly was a Christmas scene. During Fall, the leaves would change to such vibrant colors, and the town would be full of trick-or- treaters. In the summer, the local pool was open, and the kids ran the streets until the sun dropped behind the horizon, and in the Spring, you could go on picnics in the nearby woods or parks.

Pleasant Falls was a warm welcoming town. You could drive by and miss it or stop in for a burger and be on your way. The most crime the town had ever seen were local pranks by schoolkids. Maybe an out of towner would break some mailboxes. Pleasant Falls didn't have the hustle and bustle of the large cities like New York or San Francisco, and it certainly didn't have the crime – at least not until tonight.

The man on the side of the house felt his heart beat slow as he became calm with the notion of what he was about to do. His hand tightened around the rope as he ran a hand over the meat hook he had strapped to his back. Sutter Addison was a thirty-three-year-old park maintenance man for the city. If there was a park that needed to be tended to or a broken light, sprinkler head, or a busted pipe, Sutter Addison was the man on the scene. Sutter had lived his whole life in Pleasant Falls. He knew every road, every back alley, every street and rock in the town. He grew up to a mostly normal family. His father was a hardworking and well-respected police chief, and his mother was a school teacher. Sutter was given a loving home like any other average child – but Sutter had a secret, a dark yearning urge that pulled at his heart in ways he didn't fully understand as a child or teenager.

He first got the taste for this urge when he found a cat wounded on the road. It only had a small break but Sutter took fifteen minutes of pressing on the wound and making it worse before he clubbed the cat to death. There were more local cats and dogs, rats and birds. Sutter felt a strange warm feeling wash over him as he did horrible things to these innocent creatures. He felt a power wash over him. He was choosing to let them live or die. He was god.

Later when he got to high school, Sutter joined the wrestling team. He found the injuries he could inflict on other students was a rush, so much so, that he stopped hurting animals as he found humans had more emotion. Sutter liked that. Somewhere down the line, something inside Sutter had snapped. Maybe it was resentment. Maybe it was a childlike sense of abandonment that was misplaced. Envy? Jealousy? None of that. Honestly, Sutter couldn't tell you either. He was simply hardwired wrong.

His wrestling antics only lasted for so long, before he was benched permanently and forced out by the coach. He took an internship at the local morgue and also was a volunteer at the hospital. He had picked up enough basic medical knowledge plus whatever he read in books to have a fair understanding of the human body.

Sutter tried to suppress the urges, but ya know what they say about an urge. You can't keep a good one down.

Sutter had taken up boxing, weight lifting, a form of martial arts, anything to express aggression. One by one, as he let his aggression out, he was barred from these places – of course, always out of town. In a last-ditch effort to try and quell the urges, Sutter took up park maintenance. The voice in his head was always his. It wasn't like he was out of control. He didn't hear someone else talking. He wouldn't black out. Sutter knew from day one how he felt, and at first, that darkness and knowledge scared him. It would scare anyone.

Sutter had first seen her. She had a broken leg – soccer injury. He had seen it happen right before his eyes. Now, all those hidden urges, the want to hurt, the desire to be god – all of it came rushing back once he saw her bone pop out from her leg and the blood, but what warmed his blood more than anything, what made his heart pound, his throat and mouth dry and a dark arousal in his jeans – was the way she cried out.

Sutter had followed her for a few days, always making sure to have a valid excuse to be wherever he was in case she ever noticed him, always in the background watching – half paying attention to his job while he formed a fiendish plan.

Sutter had found where she lived, and tonight was his death and rebirth into something wicked, something beautiful and tragic, and most of all, something terrible.

He pried open the back-screen door and slipped into the two-story house. Sutter had cut the phone and power lines beforehand. This was his element – darkness.

He felt so at home that he opened the fridge and grabbed an apple. Sutter took a knife from the kitchen and cut a slice of apple off before placing it on the table. He wore gloves to avoid leaving finger prints. He wore clothes that he knew he could ditch and burn somewhere. Sutter had this all planned out. With every step in the house, his arousal grew, his passion and desire grew. Sutter reached the stairs and looked up. Along the wall were various pictures of her, soft blonde hair, blue eyes, sport-type of girl always smiling in her pictures. She was young. She was naïve, and she was already injured. Sutter's eyes looked like a shark's eyes. He wore a black bandana with red jagged shark teeth painted on it. The mouth of the shark was placed over where his actual mouth would be. He wore a black baseball cap that he turned backwards, black heavy work pants similar to Dickeys, a black shirt with a utility jacket, and a lightweight belt to hold his tools. He had adjusted the belt and tools to be laying against padding so they wouldn't jingle as he walked around. He wore black boots but altered the bottom slightly so they would make less noise. Slowly up the stairs he crept. Step by step, his breathing became calmer even though his breath became shallow.

His erection was pressing against his jeans. He loved everything about this. He came to his first door and froze as he looked at the hallway and his options. His hand lightly rested on the handle, and he gingerly opened the door. He saw her parents sleeping in bed, out for the count. Sutter formed a sick smile as he crept into the room and stared at them for a moment before exiting the room. He returned to the kitchen and grabbed the knife from earlier. Sutter reappeared in the room as the parents silently and peacefully slept. He took a moment as he ran his hand an inch above her mother's exposed feet. He bent down and lightly blew on them. She moved them in her sleep. Sutter stood up again and felt pride. He didn't want to wake them, so he knew he'd have to start with the father first. He would be the threat.

Without wasting a single second, he plunged the knife into the sleeping man's ribs. At the same time, Sutter placed his hand over the mouth of the father whose eyes opened as a wash of fear, panic and confusion washed over him. Sutter watched the father struggle as he dragged the knife up the length of his side. Yanking the knife out, Sutter then plunged it into the neck of the sleeping mother who was just waking up to her husband's death rattles. She almost let a scream out before she gargled blood and scrambled to the floor. Sutter kicked her in head as hard as he could and used the blunt handle of the knife to bash the father's face in. Sutter placed the knife on the bed neatly as he shut their bedroom door, leaving them to silent weep and bleed out.

The warm rush flooded his body. He felt a joyous release as he took a moment to inhale the air and savor the moment. This was what he had been needing all those years. This was what he was missing – Sutter Addison finally felt complete. He heard himself slightly panting as he caught and steadied himself, before he looked at her door. He knew it was her door because her name was written on a baby blue heart that hung on the front of the door. Sutter's eyes glossed over as he unsheathed the meat hook.

He slid her door open and found her sleeping – dead to the world. Her leg was in a cast and on her nightstand, a bottle of prescription pills, either sleeping pills or pain killers. Sutter walked over to her and took a silk stocking from his pocket. He placed the meat hook down for a moment as he lifted her arms above her head and tied them together with the stocking. She started to wake but it was no matter.

Her eyes opened to see this scene, and as she went to scream, Sutter placed his hand over her mouth. "Shh. Hush little baby; don't say a word – Mr. Nightmare's gonna buy you a mocking bird." Her eyes filled with fear as she tried to struggle and scream, but Sutter held her mouth firmly. "Now listen here. I'm going to move my hand, and if you so much as make a noise, I will kill you. I promise." Tears began to fill her eyes, and they started to run down her face. "Do you understand?" She tried to struggle, but Sutter just applied more force "Do you understand? Do you want to die?" Panic hit like a wall, and she tried to struggle. She tried to fight. She was helpless, and they both knew it. In the end, she nodded her head yes. Sutter removed his hand and watched her. She was crying and trying not to scream. Sutter turned his back for a moment, before she let out a huge cry. Sutter spun around and jammed the handle of his meat hook down her throat. "I said silent, bitch. Now you're gonna learn." The rubber and metal of the handle choked her as Sutter walked over to her dresser. He quickly opened the drawers until he found her panty drawer. He grabbed a white lacy pair and walked over to her. He sniffed them and held them over her, before he removed the meat hook – there was blood and spit on the handle. Sutter jammed the panties down her throat before slapping her as hard as he could. Her eyes filled with terror. She was still so young. She had school to go to. Prom. She had just gotten her driver's license. Emily was looking forward to college. She was looking forward to marriage and a job and raising a family. She screamed as loud and as hard as she could. Her throat was raw and sore from the meat hook handle and now the panties were making her mouth dry.

She was young to try for state. She had plans. She had her entire life ahead of her. This had to be a dream, some fever dream from the pain pills. This couldn't be real.

Emily struggled before she felt it, the cool steel of the meat hook against her inner thigh. She tilted her head forward to see Sutter playing with the edge of the hook against her soft pink skin.

"And if that mockingbird don't sing, Mr. Nightmare's gonna buy you a diamond ring." His voice was low and mocking and yet soothing. It was darkly hypnotic. Emily tried to free herself, but she couldn't. Her hands were tied. Her leg was broken. Her jaw hurt. She could taste the slight iron from the blood in her mouth and the overbearing taste of lace as her panties were rubbing her throat dry.

Sutter slowly ran the blade along her skin as he slid her shorts down. Emily began to cry as she felt the hook tip slide past her inner thighs. Her eyes were red with tears. She was trying everything in her power. Sutter slid the hook inside her and their eyes met. Hers with terror. His with pride.

"Guess that diamond ring don't shine—" She screamed as Sutter jammed the hook deep inside her and yanked up as hard and as far as he could. She screamed and shook against the bed, blood staining the sheets. Sutter yanked the bloody hook out and drove it deep into her chest and dragged it down. Then Sutter cleaned the hook off on the bed sheets and promptly left the way he came.

A warm afterglow flooded his body as his senses were heightened. He was on cloud nine. He saw her face and her eyes, the fear and terror, the panic and uncertainty behind and in them. Sutter was god to that family, and he had taken and used them. He had abused their body with steel and felt a deep orgasm rush over and inside him. Sutter Addison cut through the backyard to another street where he got into his car. He pulled off the bandana and hat as he started the engine and drove away, silent into the cool night.

Had David Brickson paid slightly more attention, this could've been avoided. Sutter Addison had seen his potential. He had felt the power and hunger subside. He felt warm and loved. Validation through blood.

That night, when Sutter Addison got home, he tossed his clothes into the wood burning stove and took a long hot shower with his meat hook. As he watched the blood flow down the drain, he masturbated himself into peace as he laid down. Hours before dawn, he fell into a deep childlike slumber. The raging storm inside him had died down for now. Sutter knew it would be back, and this time, he knew exactly how to curve and cater to it.

II

The early Autumn sun rays cut through the trees and shone gently across the sleepy town. The early morning dew on the grass made the front yards shimmer. School buses carried kids to school as people drove to work. Sutter Addison drove his truck down the street and pulled up to a park. His work day was beginning.

Today was just another day in Pleasant Falls. The horror of the night before hadn't been discovered yet, and for now, there was a beautiful life. A lie that only Sutter Addison knew.

Sutter had all the power in the world. Right now, Pleasant Falls would remain as it was until the carnage was discovered. There was a thin veil now, and Sutter had his hand on it, ready to rip it away and reveal the horror to the town. Pleasant Falls wasn't ready for that. Sutter Addison smiled to himself as he began mowing the grass in a park.

A cool breeze whispered through the trees and neighborhoods, and as the day went on, Sutter's pride only grew. With every hour, his secret became stronger in his mind. He thought of all the people standing outside the home crying, screaming, police trying to understand the scene, family and friends of the victims trying to come to terms with what had happened. He knew that once everyone saw and heard what happened, this town would be on edge. Sutter would be hiding in plain sight. He would be walking amongst the sheep – because that was what they were now. Sheep. Sutter had finally found his place in the world. His spot in the food chain had been firmly cemented now.

They were the sheep and Sutter was the wolf. He was the boogeyman of the town. He was Mr. Nightmare. The sheep were allowed to live so long as Sutter wanted them to. It was this power he held over them, and they were so blind; they had no idea. As soon as his work was discovered, he knew that the investigation would start. He knew that he had advantages on his side – he didn't leave any DNA. There were no witnesses. Sutter could freely roam, walk and stalk his next victim – and yes, there was going to be another victim. There had to be. In that dark and horrifying knowledge that he had to do it again, Sutter Addison smiled; and in that smile was a sick hunger.

The day carried on as normal right until the late afternoon. That was when the veil was ripped away.

Have you ever heard an eagle screech? Have you ever heard that raw unbridled power and force of nature? Lisa Shotwell matched the power with her own scream. Lisa was a friend of the deceased, and she had dropped by to inquire as to why Emily missed school and to see if she needed anything. When no one answered the door, Lisa went around to the back of the house and found the screen and back kitchen door pried open. Lisa carefully froze for a moment, before she went against her better judgement and stepped inside. "Emily?" she called out.

On the kitchen cutting board was half an apple, and there was a knife missing from the knife block. "Mr. and Mrs. Mason?" Her voice carried a tone of confusion. Lisa walked through the darkened home and arrived at the steps to look for her. She hugged herself as she began her slow walk upstairs. "Emily?" Her feet creaked on the hardwood steps as she finally arrived on the second floor. "Em," she called out. It was the small river of blood from under the parent's door that made Lisa freeze in her place. She hugged herself as she stared at the dried blood and dark stain on the light hardwood.

Inch by inch, Lisa Shotwell walked to the door, and as she gripped the handle and opened the door, out came the scream. It was pure panic, true unfiltered horror and shock. She stammered back and screamed as hard and loud as she could.

She hurried to Emily's door, and she gingerly opened it and fell to the floor crying. Lisa had never seen anything like it, not even in the movies. This was real. This was a mockery of the human form to her. This was sick and disgusting. Lisa raced from the house and screamed again. She sat on the soft jade grass and cried. This scene caused the neighbors to come to her aid. She couldn't speak and instead just pointed at the house. The lie was over.

Within fifteen minutes, police were clearing the scene as a sizeable crowd had gathered outside. Hushed rumors and voices could be heard mixed in with crying. From inside the house, the sheriff and her deputy stood, trying to make sense of this.

"What the hell happened. Who could've done this?" He was in shock. Deputy Mike Stevens had been a local public servant for eight years now. Together with Sheriff Lindsay Gates and the Pleasant Falls Police Department, they kept the town safe, secure and protected. Fair enough, the most crime they dealt with was domestic disputes, drunk in public, drunk driving and misdemeanors, but they were honest, fair and smart people.

Lindsay Gates stood in the hallway of the home as the bodies were packed into black bags and taken out. She ran a hand down her neck as she looked at Mike. "We need statements and a place to start. In all my years in this town, this is something else."

Deputy Mike nodded his head in agreement. "Sign of forced entry, missing knife found in the parent's bedroom," he pointed back to Emily's door, "and then that scene."

Lindsay shook her head as she walked downstairs and began a walkthrough with Mike. "Intruder pops the back door and walks in. He takes a knife from the block and heads upstairs."

Mike stopped at the kitchen island. "But not before taking an apple."

Lindsay nods her head and continues. "Intruder walks upstairs," as they turn the corner from the kitchen, they arrive at the stairs and both look up, "and then he does the unthinkable."

Mike turned to the sheriff. "Why?"

Sheriff Gates ran her hand down along her neck again as she took a step back. "That's what we need to find out. No one saw or heard anything."

Deputy Stevens looked around and took a moment before taking his hat off and running a hand through his hair. "Lindsay look, this is—"

Lindsay turned to him and agreed before he finished his sentence. "Ugly? Fucked?"

He nodded and placed his hat back on. "Inhuman. Who and why do this? The Masons never did anything."

Lindsay took a step back and glanced upstairs. "That we know of," she said.

"Let's assume they did then. What could they have been involved in to have this be the end result?" Mike questioned.

Sheriff Lindsay Gates and Deputy Mike Stevens had now found themselves leading an investigation that was unheard in this town. They had a place to start but were slightly unsure of how deep it went. "We'll run prints on the apple, the knife, the bodies…see what we can turn up."

Deputy Mike agreed as he nodded to the front door. "What do we tell them?"

Lindsay Gates looked outside at the crowd. "Keep panic down and just say the facts. We already got people spooked as it is. No need to make them worry more."

Across the street, a pickup truck had pulled up and stopped. Sutter Addison stared at the crowd outside of the house and the flashing police lights as he walked up to the house and stopped at the back line of people. In a confused and concerned voice, he quietly questioned people nearby. "What happened?"

The neighbor leaned back. "The Masons were," he paused a moment and whispered, "found. They were killed."

Sutter looked through the crowd as the coroner van pulled away. "Killed? It can't be."

The neighbor man replied, "I know, unbelievable and wrong."

That night, Sutter smiled to himself as he sat at his dinner table and ate. The wind was blowing slightly, creating a faint howl through the trees. Sutter no longer had a secret. The town was experiencing his transformation. They were in this journey together. Sutter could hardly contain himself as he shoveled food into his mouth. He closed his eyes and replayed the image in his head. The colors were so vivid in his mind. Sutter sat back and let himself enjoy the memory. Sutter carried himself to bed and laid down. He stared at his bandana and fell asleep with a sick grin plastered on his face.

As the night slowly crept across Pleasant Falls, it seemed as if the entire town was in a nightmare. Everyone seemed to sleep with one eye open and extra protection on the doors. Guns were loaded and placed under pillows. Everyone was on edge, all but Sutter. He alone knew he was safe. He alone knew that at least for tonight, the town was safe. Sutter once again held power over the town. He once again had a secret that no one else did. His dreams were that of rich and bold colors washing over him as he sat and drank from a never-ending chalice of wine.

The haunted night passed and gave way to the morbid day. The sleep-deprived town of Pleasant Falls tried to act as if the horror show yesterday was something that happened elsewhere, a million miles away from them. The citizenry and their lack of sound during their conservations made for deafening silences. The police station was running on their third pot of coffee; files, pictures, reports and prints were being run. At the center of all this chaos was Sheriff Gates standing in a conference room with pictures of the crime scene and a list of suspects. Background checks were being run on the limited leads they had. Everything was paper thin. What were the chances that Charlie, the war vet who begged for change behind Dixon's Bar, had some sort of flashback, and in the heat of the moment, butchered that poor family, or what about a stranger from out of town with a twisted mind who came from the larger cities?

Deputy Stevens walked into the room and handed the sheriff a cup of coffee as he sat down. "Thanks for this, Mike." Lindsay took a sip of the hot brown liquid as she rubbed her head and took a seat.

"We're getting the early reports back, but I think we should call out…send this up to the black suit and tie guys, ya know?" Mike sounded almost apologetic.

Sheriff Lindsay Gates leaned back in her chair as she took a long sip of the coffee and savored the taste. She closed her eyes, and for a slight second, she relaxed. Opening her eyes, she let out a heavy sigh. "I've been thinking about that option. The problem is, I'm worried that once these guys show up, they'll stir the town into a frenzy worse than what it already is. I mean, we don't know who or what this is yet." Lindsay pointed to the board, her eyes desperately scanning for something. "We call in the suit and tie guys, and they'll be interviewing everyone in the town, causing panic. People will be asking questions, and it will look like we can't protect our own citizens."

Mike took a moment as he took off his hat and ran a hand through his hair. "We already failed in protecting them though. I don't want the town whipped into some mass panic but—" Mike paused here and carefully chose what he was about to say. He took a drink from his mug and swallowed hard. "I don't know what we're doing. I was never trained to deal with this, and in all my years in law enforcement, I've only heard about these cases. What we saw in that house – I mean ask yourself, do you honestly believe we are properly equipped to handle this?"

Lindsay heard every word and she agreed to a point. "Look Mike. If I say I don't know, I may as well say no, because for this matter, they're the same thing. It's not a matter of pride or whose got the bigger badge. It's what's best for the town. We have a job outside of finding whoever did this." Lindsay nodded to the board. "We also have a duty to protect the whole town. Right now, everyone wants to go back to their normal lives. They want to wake up, have breakfast, go to work, come home, have dinner and sleep like nothing ever happened, but what they don't know is that that's a lie. They can't go back to the way things were, not as long as whoever did this is still out there, and even when we catch him, this happened. No one will forget it, and no matter if they admit or not, we'll never be able to sleep the same again. Now, if the people want normal, then it's our job to give them normal. It's our job to provide a level of maintained security and keep the peace."

The two officers stared at each other. Each had made valid points, and even now those points were resonating. Mike stared at his sheriff, his friend, and then he spoke, "At what cost? Let's say we don't go up the ladder, and this happens again and again. Then what? What's more worrying to you? Some good guys with guns asking questions and shaking things up a bit—" At that moment, there was a knock at the door. Mike went over and opened it as he was handed a folder that he quickly glanced through before tossing it down on the table. "—or some sick fuck who apparently uses a hook?" Sheriff Gates grabbed the folder and thumbed through it. She looked to Mike as he finished his coffee and held onto the door handle. "Lindsay, I respect you. You know I do. I respect this job, this town and our people. You're a friend and a colleague in the end. I'll support whatever decision you make. Just make sure it's the right call, and if you're wondering, the right call is whatever stops this from happening again." His tone was annoyance with a bit of fear. He walked out of the room, leaving the sheriff to read the report in more detail.

The sun had burned away the morning dew as the town was now in full swing, everyone working or going home or school as the bells rang out across the town. There was a question on everyone's mind, a fear in the hearts of every citizen. All save for one.

Sutter Addison sat in his truck bed eating his lunch as he watched Pleasant Falls High empty out. The students all hung out in their social circles. As a few groups of students passed by Sutter's truck, he heard the topic on their tongues. He smiled to himself, which he masked by taking another bite of his sandwich. His first work had left a deep impression with the locals. Sutter could smell the fear as the students walked by. He knew the aroma well as it was the first new smell he encountered from last night. When Emily's mother saw him and then Emily herself, the sickly-sweet sweat smell of fear rose in the air and entered his nostrils. It added to the experience.

Sutter finished his lunch and was cleaning up as he got back into the driver's seat. He saw him. Jason Murdock, the eighteen-year-old captain of the Pleasant Falls Warriors football team. Jason's arm was in a fresh cast. The injury could potentially be a nail in the coffin of his scholarship if it didn't heal right. Jason was trying to remain optimistic, and he had support from the rest of the football team, his friends and family. Everyone wanted to see Jason make a recovery and bring the Warriors that big trophy. Everyone but Sutter. As Sutter watched him, his mind now made a million jumps to things he never thought of before. This was no longer a man. This was a lion, a shark. Sutter had become a predator, and he had found his prey. The leg injury was easy. Emily was doped up. She was asleep and couldn't run even if she wanted to.

Sutter watched him for a moment. This would be a challenge. The boy would run. He could scream. Sure, he was down an arm, but he still had one. Sutter saw this not as a wounded animal limping and hiding in the middle of the herd, but a strong young buck, who despite his injury, could somewhat shake it off and fight or run. Sutter turned his radio on and drove away before he became suspicious.

The brisk afternoon turned to cool night as the town of Pleasant Falls began to lock up and load up. Hunting rifles and shotguns were pulled from safes and closets and placed near easy to reach locations. Porch lights were left on, and guard dogs were now set loose in living rooms and allowed to wander the house. As the last of the blinds were shut, Sutter knew people would be on edge. Sutter stuck to the shadows of the streets and left his truck on a main street where it wouldn't draw too much unwanted attention. He made a note to walk lightly and stick to shadows before he stopped at Jason's house. He had followed the boy home and now was scoping the area out. Sutter noticed he had a slight erection, and he smiled to himself. He took note of the white lattice vine covered panel that took up one side of the house. He took note of the window and door placement, the overhang and porch. Sutter carefully maneuvered to the back of the house and stopped when he heard a dog bark casually. The dog belonged to the neighbors. Sutter made a note and slipped back into the dark, realizing he was somewhat exposed. As he watched from the back hedge wall, he heard the neighbor's door open and the voice of a man call out as he stood on the back porch steps. There was a pause as the man called out to the pitch-black empty. After a few moments, he calmed the dog and brought him inside before closing the back door. Sutter smiled at this challenge. Everything about this thrilled him. Sutter vanished through the hedges and returned to his truck where he quietly drove off to return home and plan.

A week had passed and Pleasant Falls had returned to a level of normalcy. Maybe it was a bad dream. Maybe the tragic end of the Mason family was a onetime occurrence. The local police force had been working overtime to secure the streets. The township was just starting to recover. Everything seemed to be fine.

A storm rocked Pleasant Falls. A few districts had been blacked out due to a few blown transformers. The dark grey clouds hung overhead as the brutal wind and rain assaulted the town. Jason Murdock was sitting in the living room, watching television and nursing his arm. His parents were at work across town. Between the television sound and the rain and wind, Jason didn't hear the backdoor open slightly. Jason didn't hear it close either. Sutter stood several feet behind him. The kitchen had a clear view to the living room. Sutter wore a huge parka. The bandana covered his face as he carefully crept forward. Every step made his heart beat slow down. Sutter reached the living room as the hard tile kitchen floor turned to soft brown living room carpet.

Sutter's breath was shallow, and finally, as Jason turned to see, his eyes widened with fear. He went to scream as Sutter clubbed him. As Jason fell to the floor and landed on his arm, Sutter quickly leapt over the couch and sat on Jason's back. He placed a plastic bag over Jason's head and fastened it with a belt. He stood up and watched Jason panic. Suddenly, that sweet-sickly smell filled Sutter's nose.

Fear.

Jason clawed at the belt before clawing at the bag and ripping it open. As Jason gasped for air and tried to crawl away, Sutter grabbed hold of the belt and yanked it. Jason started to choke. His eyes watered and he gagged. Spit ran from his mouth as his eyes started to turn red. Sutter stood up and looked down. Now Jason was a wounded, frail animal. Sutter wrenched the belt up and forced Jason on his knees. Jason started to struggle less, and then suddenly, Sutter dropped the boy to the floor. Jason was coughing and choking, trying to get as much air as he could.

"Life is a frail thing. It comes and goes, and we always take it for granted, until we see just how fast it leaves us." Sutter's voice was calm and controlled. Jason tried to scream out, but his voice was hoarse and choked. He scrambled away as Sutter watched him. "You smell that? Smells like rabbit." Sutter walked forward as Jason tried to crawl to the front door. Sutter ran up and kicked him in the stomach. Jason threw up on the hardwood floor of the entryway. Sutter delivered another kick, this time to the head, a real bellringer.

"Go warriors go. Go warriors go. Go warriors go. Fight!" Sutter pulled a chain out from his belt and stood on Jason's hand. Jason tried to speak. He tried to cry out. His eyes were filled with tears. His face was red. Sutter looked down as he wrapped the chain around Jason's neck and pulled hard. The snap was final and quick. Jason's limp body lay on the floor as Sutter looked down. He had felt the death rattle, and it pleased him. That deep and shameful pride washed over Sutter Addison as he smiled at his own work. Sutter quickly opened the front door and headed back to the kitchen. He left through the back door and out into the storm. He closed the door and relocked it with his lock picking set. Out into the storm, Sutter made his way to his truck as he took off the bandana and drove down the quiet road.

The rain had let up and left the street smelling sweet and clean.

Hours later, Jason's parents stood by the front door, his mother crying as her husband held her in silence. Another crowd had gathered, and police once again saw another horrifying scene. After taking statements, Sheriff Gates and Deputy Stevens found themselves sitting back in the conference room of the police station, adding pictures to the board.

"Two attacks. Both high school students. Both athletes. Both had some form of injury." Lindsay's voice was oddly hopeful. "This is a real break, Mike. We have a pattern. We can catch him now."

Mike sat looking through the new case files. "The backdoor was lockpicked open. We found water drops and some weird kind of shoeprint in the kitchen. Whoever they are, they left that way. Jason Murdock was strangled and then had his neck snapped by a chain that was left around his neck."

Lindsay turned to face him. "He changed his pattern. This was a daytime attack. It was a boy, and there was no sign of extreme mutilation like we found on Emily Mason's body."

"Why open the front door? Why risk getting seen?"

Sheriff Gates thought about it for a moment before looking back at the crime scene photos. "Pride…they didn't take the time to clean the water that was dripping off them nor cover their tracks. There were water drops on the couch and wet marks also which shows the killer attacked while Jason was on the couch. Jason crawled to the entry way."

"The killer was mocking him?" Mike sounded disgusted.

"The killer was proud of it. They knew what they were doing. They left the door open as a sign, a warning maybe, or a calling card. The killer wanted to display this…they've become more confident. They're proud of this."

Mike ran a hand through his hair as he exhaled and sat back. "Linds, look. I know we talked about this, but we should, at least, ask for help.

The suits and tie guys do this stuff all the time. They are equipped to deal with it."

Lindsay Gates sat down across from her deputy. "I agree. I've been talking to a field agent and asked if he could come on as a consultant and side investigator. They're going to work with us, but we'll be in charge of the investigation and have this agent as a resource when we need it."

Mike let out a relived sigh. "I'm glad to hear that, but what do we do about this?"

Lindsay turned her head to the board. "Look. I know it's bad but we have a pattern now. We know who he is targeting or, at least, things to look for. That's a start."

III

The rain fell from the skies as if every drop was a tear from someone who stood by the coffins as they were lowered into the ground. Emily and her family were laid to rest in the soft wet soil of the Pleasant Falls cemetery. As family and friend said their piece, Sutter Addison watched from across the graves. He was knee deep in mud and muck. Sutter was tending to the cemetery and had to hide the sick smile that was trying so hard to form.

His work was so close and yet so far from him. He had the town by its throat and no one knew it. Sutter had two victims under his belt. Sutter Addison had finally found his place in the world. He knew exactly where he stood and what he was doing. He watched the coffins lower into the dirt. This was life. One minute they were here and alive. They had jobs and schools. They had friends and responsibilities. Then suddenly, randomly, they were snatched from the cycle of life and fed to the wolves. Sutter saw himself as the wolf. The bodies of Emily and her family were sheep who strayed into the dark. He had chosen her for no real reason other than her injury. Her family was an impulsion, a last-minute unforeseen obstacle.

Despite the fact that Sutter had made quick work of them, he didn't account for them. When he killed Jason, it was more of a challenge but the same reason and with no unintended victims. Sutter Addison felt the urge behind his teeth. He felt the passion in his blood surge through him. He had a taste of his other life, and he wanted more.

As the service ended and began to clear out, Sutter raised his head to watch them leave. He approached the graves after everyone had left, and he looked down as he quickly smiled and walked to his truck. Sutter drove to the hospital and walked inside. The smell of the sterile waiting room hit his nose as he walked to the desk.

"Excuse me." His tone was soft spoken and slow as the nurse behind the computer turned to him.

"What seems to be the problem?" She was a younger nurse with a sympathetic tone.

Sutter touched his head. "Been having trouble sleeping at night. I get headaches frequently."

The nurse handed Sutter some paperwork as she pointed to a row of seats. "You can fill this form out and bring it back. Then we'll see what the doctor can do for you, Hun." She smiled widely at him as he shot a quick smile back before sitting down.

Sutter sat himself down and took his time to fill out the chart. He stared around the waiting room, few people holding their arms or nursing legs. Sutter didn't know what or who he was looking for. He just knew it when he found it. Then she walked into the room. Sutter saw her, her sandy brown hair and soft skin. She was only on crutches. Sutter Addison saw his next challenge. He stood up and returned the paper to the nurse. "Oh thanks, Hun. You can go take a seat and we'll call you up when the doctor is ready to see you." Sutter nodded and sat back down in the packed waiting room.

She sat down with the help of a man who could've been her brother or boyfriend. The fact they interlocked hands said boyfriend. Sutter closed his eyes and went somewhere into his mind. It was calm. Before him stood a pitch-black area with a single light above his head. From the ground rose a slim, black figure with shining white eyes. The figure wrapped herself around Sutter and pressed her lips to his neck. The figure whispered in his ear, "take me."

Sutter suddenly noticed a change. His own skin had become hard and red as if he was made from some brimstone and hell pit. In one hand, he held a large meat hook, and on his head, a black crown of bones and thorns had formed. Sutter slapped the black slim figure as hard as he could, and she cried and clung to his leg before he drove the meat hook into her back. She screamed and cried as the hook was dragged up through her back to the center of her neck. Sutter left the hook in her as he took a step back and began to choke her. He felt her skin tighten in his hands as his eyes filled with a dark and ravenous hunger. She tapped his wrist, tried to breathe, but finally her body fell limp, and Sutter was alone again the dark. He snapped opened his eyes. He had an erection that was throbbing against his pants. The light from the room and outside somewhat stung for a moment, but it was the voice of the orderly calling his name back into the hospital that had snapped him out of his fantasy. Sutter quickly looked back at her and took in her form, before he vanished behind the doors.

An hour later, Sutter Addison found himself sitting in the parking lot of the hospital as the sun was setting. He had seen the girl again while he was being seen. He had lied about the sleeping and headaches. Sutter watched the doors, waiting to see her hobble out. He could almost smell her.

She exited the building with the aid of her boyfriend. He watched them as the boyfriend escorted her to the car. She was laughing and smiling. For a moment, a tinge of regret filled Sutter, but that was humanity. To regret, to mourn. To remember. Sutter would remember her this way, in the way she was when she didn't have to be anyone or anything but herself. As their car started and they drove out of the parking lot, Sutter followed at a reasonable distance.

The sun was setting in Pleasant Falls. The cool air swept down through the trees and made their branches rustle. Street by street, the streetlights flicked on as the sun set lower and lower behind the horizon.

As the happy couple pulled into a driveway, Sutter pulled up a few houses down. He had been driving with his lights off, and the couple were far too busy talking to each other and enjoying the moment to notice an atypical type vehicle and no headlights slowly following them from a distance. Sutter laid his hands on the dashboard as he watched them, her limp and his arm around her waist. Her laugh seemed to carry through the trees, and those sweet tones echoed off Sutter's ears. His lips twisted upwards into a smile.

Sutter watched them enter their home, and as the front door shut, the lights in the living room turned on. Sutter turned the key and with a rumble, the truck came to life. He switched his headlights on and started the drive back to his workshop.

Most people had homes. They had houses filled with love and food. They had memories on the walls and desks. They had warm carpets or nice-looking hardwood floors. Most people had people they returned to, families. Sometimes the family fought, but they always had each other. They had comfort and support, or they had some form of safety in their home.

Sutter had a box. An empty, cold workshop as he viewed it. His new life had taken root at home. Sutter kept up basic and common appearances, but under the skin, under the rug, in the closet and under the bed, there was the monster. The boogey man. Lurking in every shadow, around every corner was Sutter Addison. Mr. Nightmare. The Pleasant Falls Ripper. Sutter's truck pulled up to his box, and the soft soil caused his feet to slightly sink with every step toward his workshop. As he entered, Sutter quickly gathered his tools, his mask, meat hook, rope and a hammer. Stepping back out into the cold night, Sutter focused his mind. He walked to the truck and made the drive back to the neighborhood where he left the loving couple. The street was silent. Only the wind and rustle of the trees could be heard.

How long did time pass? An hour? Two? Sutter could wait. Like any good predator, Sutter knew how to wait, to bide his time, until he was sure he could get what he wanted.

The house suddenly went dark and Sutter smiled. He stepped out of his truck and lightly shut the door. Had the wind been quieter, he would've heard his feet on the soil. Stepping around the house, Sutter walked to the back door and checked it – locked.

Breaking a window would be too loud, same with trying to force the door handles. Sutter grew slightly annoyed, but that faded as he saw the basement window. He knelt down and inspected it. Having installed a few of these, Sutter knew what to do. He went back to his truck and grabbed a thin flat prybar and returned. Within moments, the basement window had been pried open and the wolf had been set against the sheep.

Sutter Addison stood up in the basement and looked around. He saw a few shelves, a washer and dryer. The light of the moon flooded the basement as Sutter walked toward the door leading up into the home. He opened the door effortlessly. Standing in the kitchen, he entered the house. As he opened the fridge, the light shone against his bandana that clung to his face. The red shark teeth seemed to almost glow. Sutter grabbed a half-eaten sandwich and finished it off as headed into the dark living room. Around the room, Sutter saw the memories on the wall, trips to sun-crested mountain peaks, grassy emerald valleys and graduation pictures that looked like a few years old.

The couple was young, high school sweethearts whose life had just come together. The house lacked expensive furniture but was clearly being built to that. The stairs had been carpeted, so as Sutter walked up to the second story, no footsteps could be heard. Sutter reached the middle of the hallway and saw an open door, the bathroom. He had been inside the home for fifteen minutes now. Sutter lightly opened a door to an empty guestroom. The only other door was at the end of the hall, and it had to belong to the happy couple. Sutter paused at the door. He listened for sounds and heard nothing.

He placed his hand on the door handle and felt it turn, panicking for a moment. There was a force on the door, and Sutter quickly let go as the door opened. The young man was standing, half-asleep and unsure of what to make of the scene in front of him. The moment his eyes widened, Sutter leapt into action. He grabbed his hammer and struck the man in the head. He let out a cry, and Sutter slammed the door shut. This woke the girl up, but all she heard was a strange noise behind a closed door.

"Aiden?" Her voice was groggy and unsure. "Aiden?" From the other side of the door, Sutter dragged him to the bathroom. Another blow to the head with the hammer kept him weak and reeling. Sutter turned on the shower and dropped the body into the tub. Aiden tried to fight back but the two hits had his vision blurry. His head ached and he couldn't focus. He thought he felt another sting on his head followed by a splash. Aiden saw red as he felt ice cold water against him. Then Aiden felt something new, a sharp burning pain in between his second rib. A hand covered Aiden's mouth. Sutter turned his head as he opened the bathroom door and stepped out into the hall. He saw the bedroom door open as the girl limped out and held onto the wall. The moment she saw Sutter's figure, she went to scream, but Sutter tackled her to the ground. She tried to fight back against him, but she was tired. Her body was resting. Her leg was limp. She never stood a chance. Sutter quickly got to his feet and kicked her in the throat as he took his meat hook and drove it into her neck. He then yanked it and dragged her along the floor to the bathroom where Aiden was. Aiden was standing slowly, and when he saw her, he tried to surge forward. Sutter slammed the door and caught his foot. As Sutter opened it again, he took the hammer and hit Aiden with it two more times. She went to cry, but Sutter dragged her down the stairs and into the kitchen where he finished her off.

The meat hook was dragged down along her neck and through her chest where he pried it out of her. Sutter Addison raced back upstairs to see Aiden hobbling out of the bathroom. Sutter took the meat hook and swung it low to catch Aiden in the leg.

Aiden's body hit the floor, and he let out a weak scream. Sutter pulled back on the meat hook and stabbed it into Aiden's stomach. Sutter dragged him down the stairs, leaving a doublewide blood trail as he yanked the hook handle hard. Blood and stomach matter oozed out of Aiden as blood trickled out of his mouth. Aiden saw her lying in the kitchen, and he reached out. The last thing Aiden saw was Sutter Addison standing over him. He saw the shine of the meat hook. Sutter finished the young man off in the living room. He returned to the kitchen and began to clean his instruments off. He took the bandana off and left via the backdoor. As he hit the street, he saw a cop car inspecting his truck. He froze and hid against the shadows of the house. Someone's must've called. He didn't know how long they had been there, but they already had to have his license plate.

Sutter went to back up as a sudden light from across the street shone on him, followed by a voice. "Hey! Freeze!" This brought the attention to the home owner and officer of whom were standing in front of Sutter's truck. Sutter darted off down the street, cutting through backyards as he heard sirens behind him and saw flashing red and blue lights dancing off the hedges around him.

"Not like this. I've only started to live." Did he say that or think it? Sutter felt waves of regret, anger, panic. He had only just found his calling. He was so young into his work. He couldn't have it end so early. To be robbed of this would be cruel. It would be tragic. Sutter heard the police from their cop car loudspeakers, yelling for him to stop. He saw house lights turning on as the neighborhood was waking up. Sutter ran to the end of the street and was out of the safe hedges. The sirens were right behind him. Sutter laughed a wicked laugh as he raced back into the hedge rows and started to retrace his steps. By now, people were coming out of their homes, and Sutter took his hammer out. As the cop car cut him off, he jumped and slid over it. One officer stepped out, and Sutter slammed the hammer against his head. The other officer went to draw his gun, but Sutter shot first, having grabbed the downed officer's weapon. Sutter put two bullets into both cops, before he got into the cop car and sped off. He was no longer safe. He was wanted. He would be hunted. Sutter Addison would have to become creative now. He sped back to his empty box, only to see two cop cars parked outside. Sutter froze before turning the silent car around and speeding off into the night.

Sutter no longer had a workshop. He no longer had safety. His face was known. His crimes would be known. Sutter Addison was about to become famous. He had killed eight people. All but two were butchered. Sutter Addison sped off into the night. Over the following days, the

Pleasant Falls Ripper or Mr. Night Terror, as the local papers had addressed him, was plastered all over television screens and newspapers.

A week had passed, and as a television shut off showing yet another image of Sutter Addison, a woman walked upstairs, and from the back porch, the back door opened, and as it closed, a meat hook lightly tapped against the doorknob.

Poezie de Groaza

I

Prologue to the Terror

I found myself in my mid-journey of life. Thirty summers had passed when the letter that would bring about my destruction would arrive in my life.

It was merely a circumstance and case of chance.

I was sitting in the sun, basking in the heat and former glory, enjoying the red of the grape when a thundering knock came from the door – beyond the parlor.

As I rose, the thundering stopped, and as I opened the door – before me sat a wax-sealed envelope with my family crest, a crest which had long since been defunct in our time. The family name and fortune had been long since spent on business deals, land, and lavish expenses.

The letter I found was the final trace of whatever title and status my family had. A death – now I am the last of my family. Bloodlines end with me.

I sat reading the letter along with several photographs and maps.

Ancestral home. Family land to be claimed by the last of the blood.

So my veins ran red as I pondered this.

Bound by blood and fate – we are slaves to the wishes of the dead and our families. Slaves to the name.

Packing the bags I needed, I called away and had a friend keep eyes over my home as I left.

The terror was calling – and I was unaware.

Through golden valley and tall tree, along seaside and cliffside, I did travel.

Off the paved road from the main towns and villages, I found the path – I had only slightly remembered this area from my youth.

As the wheels of transport battered the ground and the road became more gravel and dust, I felt ill, as if something was pulling at me. My soul. Perhaps a trick of the mind. Had I known then what I know now, I would've turned around and left. Had I known that this was the first note in a dark and tormented symphony – I would've stopped.

The house was as grand as I recalled. The estate was a huge manor. The marble statues of lions sat covered in vines as the once beautiful flower beds now were covered with a strange red vine. The fountain, which show'd Lord of the sea Poseidon, was long since dried, and the creeping red vine began to cover the base.

Rocks and gravel all along as the manor sat in silent disrepair. There was no heartbeat here.

The manor, which once held grand dinners and balls and the highest honor of guest and event, now sat in forgotten decay.

I stood in the early morning sun after days of travel to see this site, and at the heart strings did it pull. Did it pull.

Around the edges of the manor was the now overgrown hedge maze. The maze surrounded the back of the manor and the sides, and as the back led out to the rose beds and pool along with a small private family cemetery, you could always find one of the stone benches or gazebos to sit and rest in.

The manor's front was guarded by two large gargoyles, Gargouille in the native of which it resides. In-betwixt these silent protectors, there was the door, a large, solid, dark red oak with huge metal bolts and two gold dragon mouth knockers.

Producing the key from my breast coat pocket, I unlocked the door, and for a moment, I heard the manor take a breath.

The heart began to beat. I stepped into the cold and dead entrance way. On the floor was a painting of Man and Adam, fingers touching. A large, double staircase led to the respective wings of the house.

The door closed behind me. The mouth swallowed me, for I was to be the first, second and final course, yet this I did not know.

First actions. Assemble myself in a room and make the rooms that would be most use to me somewhat livable.

II

Calling of the Brood

The fire roared in the study. The rooms livable and of use to me were as follows.

Master Bedroom.

Kitchen

Study.

Library

Restroom.

These had been my rooms and areas of use. The rest sat unused and unexplored. I read up on the letters and notes left by father and fathers before, retracing the personal history, rediscovering the family tree that had been so wilted and felled throughout the ages.

Taking stock of the house and grounds, I was slowly forming a plan to make the most of this living decay.

Another heartbeat and I felt the house breathe.

Among the books and tomes in the library, I found all the classics along with some modern treasures, some folklore along with local history, family secrets and knowledge passed from generation to generation.

Photographs and pictures lined the walls and desks of these rooms and halls.

It was now when the memories came racing back. I did see the family, the Easter food and Sunday brunches. I did recall the summers and springs. A tear slid down my cheek as I felt happy. I smiled fondly at these memories for they did bring back a time of strength and vigor.

I sat in the study and allowed myself time to indulge in these savories of the past.

Of brother and sister, of aunt and uncle. Of father and mother and more.

Oh, of youth, to be nothing more than an entitled title. I longed for a return to those days.

Of simple times does the heart want. Oh, of simple times does the heart need, for I am the longing.

Another heartbeat to the core of the home.

Long into the night, I sat indulging these memories so fond.

I did call out to my family, my kin.

Join me, and so I did break the bottle and drink deeply of all it could offer me.

Long into the night, I recalled and wished for something of the past, the echo of me, the echo of the crest on the stamp.

A song and dance of the family kind, and so I dance, you dance and together we dance.

We dance.

I call the family from their graves. *Servant of the bones and blood, I compel you.*

Of ghosts and specters of old, come to me, for I am calling you.

Claw at your graves and crawl to me, zombie of blood and bone.

Red skeleton of blood and flesh, crawl to me, haunt me and these halls, for I welcome the company of my past. I call the past from the dead and beyond, for I am alone in this empty box.

Coffin crawl to accompany me down memory lane.

I howl at the full moon as the fire roars. *Rise from your graves spirits of old to embolden my spirits. I elevate you.*

Crawl to me zombie!

Feeling the clam-chill of a death-wind snake through the house, the heartbeat begins to quicken as I rattle the ghosts that haunt, haunt. Haunt me.

The red runs from the corners of my mouth and from my nose as I fall back to a chair and close my eyes.

I cry and wail into the night.

III

Visions of the Journal

The sun caused waking-life as I awoke, half-drunk from the night before. The fire had long since been smothered.

Around the room was a mess of papers and books cast from their shelves. I had suffered a tragic night. I had sense fall from my grasp as I fell into the drink and then blacked out.

Today I would inspect the manor grounds and rooms for any valuables or trinkets of note that would add to the total sum.

Room to room, I would walk, and as the cobwebs and spider webs gave away, I discover the differences and ghosts of the family. Rooms of pink and dollhouses to the map-covered walls of the more adventurous ilk, the older stale rooms spoke of the sick and ill.

The manor had been home to us all, and we left traces of us throughout these halls and rooms. Busts and portraits displayed blood greatness, and while all of this was harmless, the terror I had known existed at the back of my mind was just on the other side of the door I found myself at.

The door gave way and so I enter. I enter into a room that belonged to no known kinship.

This room existed as an office and had strange legal documents, many an odd picture and small trinket of the most curious creature.

Then – as if the unseen hand from the beyond pulled us together, I discovered it.

The journal, that once open and read, would unleash a terror and bring about my destruction.

I found the tome in an old desk – leather bound and weather worn.

Curiosity got the better of me as I read this text. The first page was a warning and welcoming.

Secrets should be buried and burned. Secrets should be forgotten and never spoken of.

Should anyone read these secrets from this text, they should terminate their life to keep hold of the knowledge inside these pages – for once you break the seal, it cannot be replaced.

As my eyes scanned the document, a lurking fear welled up in my stomach. These words spoke of paranoia and betrayers. It spoke of my family to one another; this book was a book of secrets long since rumored by the family. Blackmail. Destruction. Murder.

I should've cast that book into the fireplace and saved myself the trouble. I should've, and yet I couldn't.

The sun began to creep higher in the sky as I found myself sitting on the floor, locked into these pages.

Incest and murder, secrets and plans, secret maps for hidden rooms of the manor – all holding secrets of the family.

If my family was not already ruined, this would be the book that could surely drive and tear the family apart and shun us from history. Wolves we're all.

The sun set, and I feel as if I was dreaming. I had taken my time to study each page and letter. I had finished the first few pages and had felt comfortable in my inspection.

A gust of wind and what I thought was a voice called me to the hall – did I fall into a dream?

Was this a trick of my mind, standing and moving into the hallway – a radiant light shone down as the paintings all turned to look at me. I placed a hand against a wall to steady myself as my heart began to race.

Oh, plague dreams, why did you consume me?

Heavy, slow steps forward down that hallway of which now seemed to be growing. Vision was blurred as I could hear myself breathing – every breath making the longest draw in and out.

Was I pushed or did I fall to my knees? The judgmental glares cast down on me from the portraits of the past. I felt a thick, wet cough erupt from my chest as if I was choking on fog.

To my back as I clutched my chest to find myself staring in the eyes of the dead, its slack-jawed expression as the dead and rotting stench of the grave hit my nose – I was caused to vomit on the rug as I tried to crawl away – then the sound.

That horrible gurgling sound, the groaning. This corpse would have a meal of me. Didn't I just read something similar to this in that journal? This was a nightmare of one of my ancestors.

Did I fall asleep?

Oh, flesh thing go back to where you belong. Not of the living – I am of the living. I am of the world. You are a cold dead thing.

I felt the cold hand through my pant leg as I felt the sting of teeth against my leg. I'd kick and kick. I kicked hard against the jaw and face of this zombie. This creature of the grave.

I crawled through the hallway and choked on thick fog. I could feel it enter my mouth as I tried and failed to cry out.

Energy draining, straining. Vision blurred, heart beating slowly as I bled out on the rug, the mocking expressions of the paintings around me. I am small.

Did I fall asleep or was I awake? Was this my dream?

I awoke with the midday sun; my skin was warm as I found myself rising to my feet in the hallway of my dream. Nothing was out of place – a fever dream of terror. Nothing more.

A trick of the mind.

Inspection of my form showed an intact body, yet it felt so real. Little did I know, this was the first of the fever dreams that would soon consume my mind.

I walked back into the room and reread the journal – the detail of the dream was gone; instead it was a similar dream...or was it the same dream and in my sleep, I had merely given it a stronger presence than it had? I closed the journal for now and left it on the desk as I got dressed and stepped outside.

IV

Confession of Secrets

I sat on a bench in the middle of the garden maze. I sat and stared up at that big blue overhead.

The last few days had left me out of sorts, and I had to be honest – I had to tell myself the truth. Finally, it was time for an omission.

We – my family. We were the reason for our downfall. So hard did we keep to high society. We tried to hold together, yet the cracks were deep and we did nothing to repair them.

Forced inbreeding against a few select members of the family by some of the darker family members had caused deep and savage cracks, and yet we didn't speak up for fear of what would happen.

I ran away from title and name before the rumors spread to me as well.

A wellspring of vices helped drain the money, addiction to skin. Drink and narcotic would finish off the rest.

Deeper carnal pleasures would morally bankrupt the family.

Here I sit, the last of my family, sitting under that pale blue sky as I wonder why we do the things we do.

Why am I the way I am? Am I the product of this forsaken family? Forsaken family for I am nothing more than man. I have ruined and sat and watched the ruin of my family and did nothing to help stop it.

I am as bad as they were. Wolves we're all.

The mind wanders to a time in my early twenties — there he stood. A strapping young man with muscles and form. He was bleeding at my feet. This was how I would entertain myself, pugilism, fist to fist. He was being paid good money — or at least, so he thought. He let the cash go to his head, and although he was in top form — he wasn't ready for the fight.

I was willing to die, to bleed out. I was willing to let go, and so I fought tooth and nail. He didn't. My fists were covered in his blood. He was coughing. Some of his teeth had fallen out. His body was bruised and he was beaten. I looked down at him in pity.

He looked to me in defeat — it was that look that made me take his life.

He was pathetic in this state, and this is who he really was.

The match, I knew no one would stop it. I sat on his chest and slowly and methodically beat his face and nose, until the crowd stopped cheering. A silence fell across the barn as I stood. Long, thick strings of blood ran from my hands as the crowd turned their eyes from me — I collected my winnings and tossed them onto the body of the dead boy.

I left feeling better about myself. There was no regret then. There was nothing.

I had killed in cold blood.

I was the wolf, and he was the rabbit. I saw the fear and pity in his eyes. He was helpless against me. After that, they stopped allowing me into rings. I had been barred from the fight scenes, and so I left that vice behind.

Here, now years later, I thought of that man – the boy I killed. One hand touched the other, and I looked down – oh how alive I was and felt.

Vices die hard – I know what needed to be done. On the grounds of the manor, there was a family chapel – a stone and woodwork of truly Gothic architecture.

Walking out of that hedge maze, I found my way to the chapel – the door opened slowly as I stepped into the sanctum. The holy water in the basin was green and thick slime.

Hanging on the wall in near perfect condition was the cat-o-nine-tails. I grabbed its handle as I walked toward the statue of our Lord on the cross.

On bended knee, I removed my shirt and closed my eyes.

To purge the sin and shame, I offer in blood and flesh.

The crack of the cat and barbs pulling and yanking my skin and flesh, pleasure and pain for I must pay for my actions – as my family did before me.

I shed the shame as I slightly whimper as I feel my back burn. To pay and repay for blood amount, I can never repay, yet I can start the collection. The debt collector is in.

Slap after slap after slap after slap after slap after slap.

The flesh is torn from my back. I am mortal man – now blood on the floor allows the heart inside the manor to beat more.

I give life to the death and allow the dead to come back and live through actions of myself – for I am the last. I am the last.

Time lost is something gained – but I am unsure of what I gained from my time spent in the chapel.

I stand and place the now well-fed cat back on the shelf. The sun had begun to set – how long was I in the chapel – my back stung as the cloth stuck to my skin. The blood ran through, and for a moment, I took pride in the pain.

To my knees I did fall. To my knees I did fall. The suns final rays caught me in awe as the golden light slowly faded behind the pine tree line.

I was now in the dark of the night. The moon had washed the scene in her pale soft tones.

Dance of the moon – so I stood and felt the sting of cloth on wound. I bled – I bled. Arms out and failing. Here again, from my lack of blood and lightheaded, I was swept into a dream – the gargoyles did dance and join me in a sinister ritual dance.

Glory to the moon and her children, unchained and swallow the sky – come O Great Wolf and consume.

The gargoyles snickered as they praised and howled to the savagery, mocking faces at my pain. My cries for joy became cries of woe.

Cast down to the gravel, I grovel.

The gargoyles did return to their posts as I humbled my way to the stone steps and red oak door.

To my feet I rose and spied across the silent tree line – images of my family before me now haunted my eyes as I opened the door. I heard a heartbeat.

Froze fast, I stood my ground and closed my eyes. Hand against the wall and I tried to focus on the heart beat – the beating of the drum. The heartbeat is my heart.

The stinging of the cloth – I take it from my back and cast the red on the floor.

The heartbeat fades, or is it a trick of the mind?

I trudge back to the study and light a fire as I open a bottle of red.

Idly staring into space as my hand cradles the bottle – at nothing I stare.

V

Haunting

The following days were spent the same, shedding blood and skin, reading over papers and documents – and from that accursed journal.

My dreams had become waking nightmares, and so I did not sleep.

My health had started to wain as food had been replaced by drink – anything to keep those damn dreams from me.

The passages from that journal were not for the sane eyes – headaches started to occur and lapses in my memory and judgement.

I would read a passage from that book – I would become agitated and lose time – lose track of time.

The passage I would reread later would be misremembered, which would only inflame my rage.

The book is always just a few steps ahead of me. Mocking me – to madness.

These headaches worsen as I am kept bound by the page, hanging onto every word as if some unseen force drove me onward into this vile volume of verbiage.

I am haunted by the past – even past that does not belong to me. Blood memory causes me to feel empathy for those who have long since passed away.

From the manor's guts somewhere deep in the stomach of the estate, the heart began to thunder. It began to rumble and beat.

The waking house brought about the ghosts who sleep in the rafters and shadows. Who and what lurks beneath the stairs and corners of the room – they creep and begin to slowly choke out life where it can be found.

Did I fall asleep or am I awake?

From the skies came an awful screeching of what sounded like bats – howls of pained ancestors on winged messengers.

Is this a fever dream waking?

Am I from the beyond or is this worse?

Beat, beat, beat, beat, beat, beat, beat, beat, beat. Beat the walls of the rooms. Claw at the mirrors and shatter them to provide me an exit, an exit away from this dream.

My head is pounding as the full weight of my ancestry brings down torment all around me.

The beating heart of the house now echoes off every room – the manor begins to breathe a fated heavy breath.

Every clock is ticking in rhythm as I begin to lose my time, to lose my mind, to slowly lose track of what is happening around me. Poltergeist of mine – allow me rest. I cast you from these walls and yet my cries do nothing.

I am forced to move – I run out to the garden as the precession of kin follow and circle me.

I dream of a bloodletting festival – a meal of penance.

The serpents of overbearing mothers, aunts and grandmothers coil around me as the pressure from the Patriarchy look down with disappointed gazes.

Be gone sprits of old. Return to your graves and rest. Bother me no more for my soul is pure.

I am pure – I scream out into the night.

Did I dream or am I waking now?

In the study, I awake to the morning sun. Half-blinded by the rays, I stumble to my feet. Has it been days or weeks? Has it been months? A year?

What was I doing in this manor – why did I come here? I threw myself down and felt a sharp, jagged sting take my back. The shirt was stained with blood as I looked in a full-size mirror to reveal a back heavily whipped and scarred. The cat sat next to the chair – was this my device?

To punish myself inside? The journal sat open, halfway finished – I grabbed the text and saw that, to my horror, I had been revising and editing the book. Huge red lines and words were taken in and out – removed and moved around.

Who had done this?

Was this my device?

What time was it?

Was it the sun or moon that had woken me? Both seemed to be the same.

I fall to my knees, exhausted. Making my mind up – day or night, whatever it was, sleep was best now.

I hauled myself to the main bed chamber and threw myself down onto the soft sheets.

Spinning as the walls seems to inch forwards ever so slightly – just enough for me to choke on the thinning air. I sit up and catch my breath as I feel a sudden weight on my chest.

Vile tormentor of the dreamscape – I expel you!

Did I dream or am I awake?

Suddenly!

The ticking of a clock echoes off the walls as I hear my own heartbeat, and as I cover my head and close my eyes, suddenly, it all stops.

VI

Beating Heart

Suddenly!

The visions and noise ceased to be and I fall into awake – or sleep.

My eyes open later and I stand, exhausted, drained of blood, sore and hungry.

Carefully, I shuffle my feet toward the door and into the hallway – silence.

Was this a trick of the mind?

I feel anxious no longer. As if on the first day of arrival – I feel peace.

To the kitchen, I make my way as I grab a bottle, various cheeses, meats and breads – the sun looks low on the starting horizon. Early morning.

It would appear that whatever ghastly infestation residing in my ancestral home has taken rest and allowed me to recover – if only for a moment. It is welcomed.

Once I had food in the belly, I took to the library and began to delve into the estate blue prints.

The idea had come to me in the final seconds of torment before sleep found me.

I would explore and destroy the heart of the manor – tools gathered from the day and a plan was drawn out.

Into the bowels of the estate – I would confront this beating heart and rip it from the core.

I kissed the sun goodbye as it vanished, and night gently lay down in its sweet presence. I found the large basement door at the back of the main room – a large ornate oak and steel door. I slid the skeleton key into the lock, and the door unlocked – a bated breath and I could feel the heart shutter.

Lighted torch and down I go.

The staircase down was a short walk and soon my feet rested on the stone and dirt ground. Wine racks sat unused and dust covered. The chatter and squeak of rats and other things scurried away from my light.

Lighted torch in one hand and service revolver in the other – onward I press.

The air is thick, moist. Every step underground and I feel a force pull back on me. The echo of my own breathing becomes louder. My vision strains.

For ages, I seem to walk into the dark underground. I lost hope to see the sun – I would do what my blood never could.

If I die, I shall take the heart with me.

The red vine returns. So deep underground and now on closer inspection, I see it is not just a vine. It's a vein, and its alive.

The walls and floor are covered, and the vine lines the walls and ground – I hear the beating return slowly, slowly and softly.

Into the dark, I follow it. With every step, the beating becomes louder. The vines and veins become thicker – I walk into that dark hallow – the torch shows the impossible sights around me – suddenly, to my gaze comes a door – which was not there on the blueprints – I hear the heart.

I open the door and see the heart.

It's beautiful.

Every detail was in vivid real life – this was not a trick of the mind.

Awestruck, I close the door and walk near it – the heart beats slower for a moment as if to shy away from my touch.

I holster the revolver and lightly place a hand on the heart as it throbs and pulses.

A tear of joy and beauty falls from my face and I clench the heart—

I rip it from the core, and suddenly, I feel the ground shake before me – I hear another worldly wail as I tear and shred the heart from its cables and veins. The heart beats rapidly in my hand, and suddenly, the walls begin to rattle and crack

Retracing my steps, I run through the dark as I hold the heart close my chest. All around me, the quake brings about the walls and ceiling.

Closer to the surface I return, and as I kick the door open and break into the main entry way, I see a parade of ghosts – my blood.

They cry and scream as if in hellfire agony.

The sight of the heart causes them to cry and scream – the haunted now becomes the tormentor for I hold the power. Surging out into the courtyard, the house crumbles in sections as the gargoyles scatter from their posts.

High in my hand, I hold the heart to the sky and I shed tears – I break for this – none of this was a trick of the mind.

I look at the beating heart in my hand, and for a moment, I feel pity—

For a moment.

Gripping it with both hands, I shred the heart in two as the manor shakes and falls into dust and rubble before me. A violent and traumatic shake forces my family home to the ground as I give one final tug into the heart and cast it to the ground- - suddenly, I seize my chest. I fall to my knees.

Destruction promised.

As I close my eyes, the last of my strength goes, and I fall into a permanent sleep.

Death comes from us all—

As I fall, my chest against the ground before my once proud manor, now nothing but bricks and stone of rubble and final decay.

And yet there is a heartbeat.

There was a heartbeat.

It Wakes

Don't turn the lights out for that's when it wakes.

"Can you leave the light on?" This request was always at the front of my lips when the sun would drop. My dear mother and understanding father bought me a nite-light to fend off the dark. What they didn't know was that my cries for help and the power of that little Superman nite-light were actually something far more real.

Some people just hit a streak of bad luck – when this thing found me, I instantly knew fear. I was six-years-old when I first encountered it. It was during a heavy rain storm, and I could hear the wind forcing the trees along the side of the window – a lightning strike revealed to me the thing that would stay with me for the rest of my life.

Clinging to the window, getting assaulted by the storm was the…well, I call it "Grey." Allow me to describe it.

Grey is about four-feet. He has a thin black frame with huge, lightbulb grey eyes. His fingers are long and have huge nails. His mouth is always pulled back into a large Cheshire-like grin which exposes his jagged and crooked teeth, which, by the way, are many – Grey's teeth start humanoid enough, but the points turn into shark teeth, and he constantly drools and slobbers on himself.

He wheezes and hisses – just low enough so I can hear him. He wants me to know he's there – waiting.

Grey hates the light – so much so that once I woke with Grey sitting on the edge of my bed. I felt his claws plucking and tugging at the blankets near my feet. I awoke to him beginning to lean over me – the battery in my nite-light had died. I quickly started screaming and my parents rushed in. As soon as the light from my light turned on, Grey ran under the bed. He moved too fast for my parents to see. They let me sleep in their bed that night. The next night, I sat and watched Grey nurse and lick his wounds in the corner of my room – he sat glaring at me. The light had burned his skin. It was from that moment on I started sleeping with a flashlight under my pillow.

The years went on, and from childhood to high school, to college and my first jobs to my own place, to my girlfriend and now wife, grey has stayed with me.

Over the years, I tried to confront him, but it never worked. Grey would always scurry away. I'd set traps for him that he would narrowly scurry out from. All this attention had made Grey quite angry with me, and now, I know he craved to feast on me.

I'd found that removing the frame from my bed and using the box spring would force Grey to become creative – something it wasn't so great at.

With no bed to hide and cover under, Grey would have to find a porch to scurry under. He'd have to find a low table to hide under, dark corners. Sadly, this trick only lasted as long as I stayed single as no self-respecting woman would allow it. Grey would always come back after I got with a girl, and my bed returned to a more traditional setting. Of course, I could never tell anyone about Grey – who would believe me?

This is the stuff that kids go through – not an adult.

I feel like Grey knew it too. It would mock me. After years of abuse, I thought I would end this. I thought I would finally end what Grey was up to. I didn't know anything about it. I didn't know what it wanted or where it came from. I didn't know anything about Grey. There was and still is no history on it. So, I figured why not set the stage for the final confrontation.

My girlfriend was going out of town for a few days to visit her sister. I would be alone, well…not really. It was going to be Grey and I, and I had enough. I woke in the early morning to see my girlfriend off and then I set to work. I replaced all the light bulbs with high power, non-energy saving bulbs and moved their placement throughout the house. I made trap points of light and hid heavy-duty LED flashlights through the house. I made the bed up extra nice for Grey. I even put the bed skirt on – something my girlfriend had always wanted, but I never allowed *for obvious reasons*. I spent the day making the house exactly how I wanted it. The final touch was one pistol in the nightstand, a shotgun in the hallway – that was now a wall of light with the flick of a switch.

I added another sheet on and folded it in such a way I could quickly grab it and throw it over Grey. Then with a simple twist, I could turn it into a sack and contain it. The plan was perfect – I had him.

The sun was dropping low in the sky. Dinner came fast, and I finished up and started shutting off the lights in the house. With every light, I could almost feel those grey bulbous eyes glaring at me. I lay in bed and closed my eyes – I did not sleep.

It seemed like an eternity. I was white-knuckled – never had I confronted Grey before. Not like this.

I began to lose the edge. I got relaxed. The pillow was like a nice cold cloud that fit my head perfectly. The bed was perfect. I stretched out, and as I did, my foot slipped out from the cover – this is when my fear returned. As my foot left the warmth of the covers before I could retract it, I felt a long, cold nail drag across my warm foot. I froze.

How long had he been there?

I had the sudden urge to move, to scream. He had been watching me sleep, edging closer every second. My hand tensed as I fought the urge and lay still. Slowly, my hands gripped the covers, ready to spring and start the steps to Grey's downfall. I felt a pressure on the bed, no more than a large cat – I heard the hissing and felt Grey slowly working his way up my body over the sheet. When I felt his long, slimy, snake-like, ice cold tongue against my neck, I sprang into action. I screamed as loud as I could – which startled Grey. It tried to reel back, but I threw the sheet over him and twisted it, similar to how a snake handler nets a snake. I grabbed the pistol from the bedside table and hopped to my feet. I could hear him snarling. As his claws started to shred the sheet, I fired three shots into the center mass of movement – apparently this only angered him. I saw black blood ooze through the sheet though. The old rule applies.

If it bleeds, you can kill it.

Grey shredded through the sheet and leapt to the celling, then down on me. As it went to slash my chest, I fired two more rounds into Grey. The bullets sank into his skin as black ooze spurted out and onto me. Grey recoiled, and I grabbed the flashlight from under my pillow. Turning it on, Grey raced out of the room. I checked the gun and headed into the dark and quiet house.

I saw traces of ooze, the flashlight lighting a path for me to follow slowly into the kitchen, and I saw Grey scurry across the floor. I hit the switch, forcing him from the room and into the living room. I didn't want to fire wildly – this had to be aimed and make direct contact. Grey was fast, and now the stakes were known. Only one of us was leaving alive. Grey raced up close and slashed at my wrist, leaving pain and blood as I dropped the gun. I saw grey start crawling toward me, and for a moment, I thought this was it. I stumbled back into the hallway with Grey lurking near. As Grey stood in the middle of the walkway and my back hit the backwall, I grinned. "Fuck you!" Grey ran toward me at hearing me say that – I reached up and grabbed the shotgun as I hit the light switch. My eyes burned as the hallway flooded with light. Grey let out a horrible, unworldly shriek. With my eyes closed as I staggered back, I blind fired. A shotgun at close range inside a narrow hallway space can do a lot of damage – I had him. The sound of the gun going off echoed off the walls, leaving the smell of a freshly fired gun. I slumped against the wall as I heard crying.

Grey could vocalize? I slowly stood up as I heard a female voice crying and whimpering. I opened my eyes slowly and staggered forward— "Oh god no!" I dropped the shotgun and raced to the start of the hallway— "Ash?"

Ashley was lying on the ground crying; her chest was soaked with blood and buckshot. She looked at me confused and scared. I held her in my arms. I was as confused as she was.

"I fee-I feel…cold," Ashley cried softly as she shook and her grip tensed on my arm. Then she fell back into a restless, forever sleep. With my tears in my eyes, I looked up into the dark living room to see Grey wringing his claws together and his sick grin.

Ashley had come home early as her sister's apartment was being fumigated on a last-minute notice, so Ashley thought she'd just come back rather than shack up in a hotel. She had no idea about Grey, the light, the gun. She had no idea of any of this. She had just got caught up in my mess.

"Very good. That's progress." The doctor smiled at me as I sat in a chair across from him.

"Doc, you gotta believe me…I was aiming at Grey…"

His look was empathetic. "I understand you were aiming at Grey, but what you need to tell yourself is that Grey is just in your mind, a childhood fear that you let run wild."

Those words stung. I didn't belong here. I handed the doctor the rest of my journal – my daily journal for my therapy. Apparently, if you murder your girlfriend in a paranoid, accidental shooting and claim it to be the reason of hunting a bed monster, you get sent here – Pleasant Falls Hospital. Home for the psychologically injured and recovering.

They told me Grey was all in my head. They said he was all made up. It had been like this for months now. Her family never forgave me. My family were trying to be supportive. None of it mattered.

I was led back to my room, and I lay down. The sun set below my window, and I closed my eyes. That stinging feeling, the knot in my stomach – was I crazy? I mean, after all, I've never found any research on Grey. I've never found anything close to it online or in books – it's all been folklore.

I closed my eyes and cried as I thought about Ash's beautiful face, her eyes staring into mine.

The sun set and I sat alone in my room, cell – whatever you wanna call it. I turned on my side and began to fall asleep.

I cried myself to sleep, and as I did, I heard a hissing from under the bed. Now it was just Grey and I.

Rending the Veil

I

Another night as she coils around me. I feel her cold breath against my skin. Her coils wrap around my exposed body. Snake charmer.

I know this is a damned dream, one that haunts me in the early waking hours. Oh, I have seen the light – I have seen for miles. My erect member rubs against her coils and my thigh. She drags her split tongue down along my neck as I try and recoil in abject terror. I cannot move. I am simple, her food, so she should choose.

Suddenly, I come to and I'm alone again in the dark of my room with the ticking of the clock, thundering throughout the apartment. My eyes hurt, for the wonderous and horrifying visions they have seen, and cannot comprehend the world behind the world, and yet I know, they are there. In the dark of our world, headache throbs as I vomit to the side of my bed. The bile and stomach acid erupt from my mouth as I hunch over and expel onto the hardwood floor. I see a dying cockroach in my vomit as I stare out of that brick loft window and out into the shining, rising, burning sun.

The sun saves me, and yet, in the final edge of darkness, I see the final trace of the hidden world fade for the day. The tentacle of the mass slides away – shying from the light.

I pass out on the floor into a restful sleep.

The banging of my door wakes me sometime later. Groggily, I walk to the door and open it to see her, the woman next door to me.

"Hey, I brought you this." She holds up a cheesecake. I smile as I welcome her in.

"Hey Sarah, thanks." She walks in and sits down on my sofa. She clocks the vomit and gives me a look of pity.

"Another rough night?" She offers friendship.

I sit down across from her as I place a coffee mug in front of her with a slice of cheesecake for each of us. "No more than usual. I just get bad turns at night."

Shrugging out of empathy, she takes a sip of the coffee "I hear sometimes, its ok, ya know. My younger brother used to have night terrors – they're pretty tragic."

"Tell me about it." I nod my head in reply as I take a sip of coffee and sit back and rub my temples. "Hey, Sarah – what time is it?"

"Five-thirty. What time did you ace out last night?"

I hold up a hand and shake it from side to side. "Pick-a-time O'clock."

"Ethan, maybe you should see a doctor? A specialist or someone?"

I raise my head to look at her and lower my shoulders as I sink into the chair. "I tried all that when I was a kid. Parents put me through tests and meds. Doctors looked me over and inside. I'm just suffering from a bad case of the 'unable to sleep' nights. It cost them a lot of money – money that I don't exactly have."

She gives me a look of understanding, and she takes a bite of the cheesecake, and for a moment, she gets lost in the taste. I follow suit, and we sit in silence, just smiling at eat each other like kids.

This was our little ritual – cheesecake and coffee.

Sarah was a West Coast girl, born and raised. I was a Midwest boy – what more was to be said?

We both found our way to colder shores and East Coast skylines. Being the "out of towners" and happening to live a few doors down from each other, we naturally found a mutual friendship in the fact that this scene wasn't our natural environment. I worked for the building we lived in – maintenance and janitorial services. In return, it came with a nice little rent-controlled room at a slightly discounted price. Sarah worked for a news station and fact checker. She helped write the news teleprompters. So, a tiny but important cog of the twenty-four-hour-news cycle.

We sat in silence just enjoying our coffee and cheesecake, making idle chitchat. Sarah and I kept similar work hours – which added another level of friendship since night and third shift workers didn't have the biggest social circles. Sarah was heading out to work, and I was about to start my rounds. We said our "see ya laters" as she hit the road to work, and I hit the shower.

I turned the water on and stepped in.

The hot water seemed to wash away any remaining trace of last night that the coffee and cheesecake may have missed. I closed my eyes and stood under the therapeutic manmade waterfall.

I closed my eyes and seemed to fall into a dream. The sound of the water started to echo off the walls. From the other side of the clear plastic shower curtain, I saw it emerge from the fog.

Out of the thin mist came the crawling thing. It normally stuck to the ceilings of my loft at night.

It was a slender, black and blue featureless figure. It crawled low to the ground like a lizard of sorts. It could be called something out of a nightmare.

It reminded me of a Venus flytrap, and from the interior of the mouth, octopus like tentacles were moving with an air of sentience. The head rose and inhaled as if it was tasting the moisture from the room. In awe and fear, I stared at this thing – I had no name for it.

What would you call fear manifested?

I felt myself release into the water out of fear, and having the slightest tinge of ammonia in the air, for a moment, caused the thing to tilt its head in confusion as it lurched forward and put its claws on the edge of the porcelain tub. The thing crawled into the tub and recoiled for a moment at the water. It stood upright and looked down at me. I knew not where its eyes were, nor if it could see or hear or just sense things. Changes in the air maybe? It raised its head and the flytrap opened. Black strings of gunk oozed down from the trap and slid onto the shower floor. The tentacles seemed to explore the area. I closed my eyes and slowly counted to ten – I was trying to keep calm, but I knew I was losing it. Suddenly, I think I felt it?

A nosebleed. I stumbled back and heard a sudden noise and commotion. As I opened my eyes, I saw the thing scatter and fade into the fog. The back of my head hit the wall as I snapped to and regained balance. A tinge of red fell to the floor as I wiped the blood from my nose. They were getting worse. I shut the water off and stepped out into the foggy bathroom. I began to dry off as I wiped the fog from the bathroom mirror. I was thrown back by a shock – the thing was in the mirror and snapped at it. It shattered the mirror, causing shards of glass to fly out into the room and my body and face. I was shaking as I felt myself choke, cough. I tried to move. I struggled to hold myself up as I threw up into the sink. I slowly raised my head to see the intact mirror.

Call it par for the course.

II

I set out to my work, head slightly spinning as I walked down the hallways, checking on the hallway fire extinguishers and fire escape doors, elevator doors, floor by floor checking to make sure everything was within code. I always started at the roof and worked my way down.

The basement and boiler room were my last area to work in. I hated it down there. I took the elevator up to the roof and began my perimeter scan. I checked some breakers and a few other technical things. I took a lungful of air and stared out across that New York skyline. The brisk air filled my body and for a moment, for a slightest of second, I felt the horror and aches of my body leave. The air was brisk and had that sour-city smell. I stared across the city and saw it, the building from this morning.

The one with the tentacle that was dragged away by the sun.

It was there now – I couldn't see it right there in that moment, but I knew it was there. In truth, it was always there. The world behind the world was always there.

Some people think it's magic, dragons, unicorns. They think it's ghosts and God. They think it's werewolves and vampires. They want to believe it to be aliens and wizards.

I've seen behind that thin and frail veil.

You're all wrong.

Lovecraft was close. He was the closest we knew to being right.

What lurks behind the world. What lurks just around the corner, sharing our world, sharing our streets, showers, shadows, cars, houses. The world before our world was something much more arcane. Older…with a much darker intent.

I shuttered at the thought as I went about my work. Floor by floor I checked on cracks in walls, door handles. The hours ticked away as my iPod provided the soundtrack to this nightly shift.

I came to my office and checked the security cameras with the security guards, Rick and Patrick. They were two nice guys, local to the area. We took lunch together, and they watched my back from the cameras. Soon it was time to face the fact that I had done my rounds, from the top to the bottom…and now the horrid basement. I swallowed hard and opened the steel door. The basement and boiler room were modern, well-lit and maintained.

That didn't stop it from royally freaking me out. A typical life with an average amount of horror movies and urban legends, a childhood fear of the dark, a tinge of claustrophobia and there you have it. The chemical formula for being freaked out by basements and boiler rooms.

I stepped down and reached the concrete floor and looked around at the well-stocked shelves and the inventory for the building. Honestly, there was nothing to be scared of. I was being childish. I went about my nightly duties and doubled checked the inventory, filled out order forms for supplies and had a pretty uneventful hour or two. I checked in with Rick and Patrick as I made my way back up the stairs. That's when I froze.

Something grabbed my leg on the stairs. I felt the fingers wrap around my ankle.

I tried to scream, but instead I looked down just in time to see this deformed humanoid yank at my leg. I shifted my weight to shake free and fell down the stairs back to the base floor.

This hunchback dog-faced humanoid ran to me as I jumped to my feet. It was slobbering and slathering, trying to claw at me with its deformed hands. I kicked it in the side, and it let out a sort of restrained yelp. The dog-faced humanoid charged me with anger. I was able to push it into the wall behind me as I simply moved out the way. It turned away and ran into the dark. I darted for the stairs, and as I reached the door, I felt the stairs give away.

Was I floating or falling? Suddenly I found myself short of breath, and as I closed my eyes and tried to count to ten, my eyes were opened by the extreme shining light.

I found myself in a massive church with angel statues, yet the faces of the angels were not that of the divine nor of men.

The faces were horror dog-faced, gargoyle-like, squid form and other various creatures of the abyss. The horror and shock sent me reeling as I made my way for the front door. I put my weight behind my shoulder as I shouldered the door and burst past it. Night fall.

I found myself in a strange cityscape. The buildings were tall and slender. They were slightly twisted and all had pointed roofs. The streets were narrow and stone. There was a fountain which depicted the union of man and some horrible nameless thing. Slime green water was pouring out from it.

A bell sounded somewhere, and I saw doors to the buildings fling open. From these strange towering homes and houses, the residents took to the street after the call of the bell.

They were humanoid dog-faced things. They were hunched over, some on all fours, some upright. Some clung to walls and crawled along the surface. All manner of spider, fly, crab and dog humanoid traveled in silent strict order to the call of that thundering bell. The top of the church, which caught my attention as the source of the bell, had something looming atop it.

It was a large, tentacled mass, a bulk of flesh and matter that clung to the side and top of the church. I noticed that there were a few of these huge creatures scattered around the town. One of the nameless things bumped into me, and I screamed involuntarily – but the ringing of the bell clearly had some sort of power of these things. For even though they knew I was there – none seemed to notice, or if they did, none would dare break away from the march into the church. I backed through the crowd as the last of the citizens were welcomed into the church and the doors were slammed.

I heard a wheezing laugh as I turned and saw an old man with heavy bandages around his eyes. He sat with a cup. His skin was grey and withered. "I can smell you traveler." I froze as he let out another wheezing laugh. "I'm blind, not senseless. Come take a seat. I'm about the only friendly thing here."

Against my better judgement but having no real other option, I took a seat near him. My voice was one of concern and confusion. "What is this place?"

The old man scratched his beard for a moment as he looked in my direction. "You don't know where you are? Traveler, you have come a long way to get this lost."

"Look, my name's Ethan. I'm from New York. I was working and then some weird dog thing attacked me. I fell down the stairs and I ended up here...wherever this is."

The man took a moment to ponder my words. "You're in the Valley of the Pale."

"The wh— Look man. Can you stop speaking in riddles? Where the hell am I?"

The old man laughed as he tilted his head. "Traveler, the pale is the world before your home. It's a world before the bibles of the world, before the gods of the world. The pale is where reapers are born. It's where the myths and legends hear their myths and legends. The Valley of the Pale is timeless, ageless, and forgotten. If you're here, it's not by mistake."

I stood up to walk away "Where you going, Traveler?"

Anger filled my voice. "Look, I'm lost. I'm scared, and I'm angry. If you're not going to help, you go screw. I'm going home."

The man wheezed as he relaxed against a wall. "Traveler, where is home? You don't even how you got here. How do you expect to get out?"

He had me. I was angry but he was right. I didn't know what this place was, what to do or where to go. I sat down, and I'm sure he could sense my anger.

"Traveler, you need to be mindful of what you see. Sight leads to the grave discovery of things better left unseen. Somethings are made to only be thought of and left alone to the eye." He tapped his bandages and wheezed as he pointed at the church "You know what's happening in there?"

I looked to the church but dared not think about it.

"Blood rituals, sacrifices, witch burnings—" He wheezed with pride. "This whole place is under the law of fear and curses. Purge your skin. Admit your sin." He tapped his bandages. "I saw too much, and so I offered my sin to the city, so that I can rest."

"You did that to yourself?" I was worried, and my fear was rising.

"Traveler, after all the things I done seen in the Pale, this was the best thing to happen. I witness nothing now and am therefor free of the horror of this place."

I heard his words but couldn't and wouldn't believe them. This was something far worse than I thought. I had a million questions, but they felt like bullets in my mouth. The old man didn't wait for me.

"Traveler, you ought to be returning. From water we rise to water we sink." As he spoke, rain started to pour down throughout the city of The Valley of Pale. "Traveler." He raised his hand and placed it to my head. I tried to object, but before I could, he jammed his thumb into my left eye. I screamed as I shut my eyes and fell back.

"Ethan!" I woke up shaking and trembling. Patrick and Rick had found me. I was in the basement. "Ethan, you're alive man! You started shaking or something like you were having a seizure." I slowly sat up and tasted bile. My eyes hurt. My stomach hurt. I felt dizzy and confused. Patrick was standing as Rick was kneeling over me. "It looks like one of the stairs may have had water or something on it. You slipped and fell. You've been out of contact for an hour and we haven't seen you on cams. Are you alright?"

I reassured them I was alright, but I had to ask myself, *Was I alright?* It was time I took Sarah's suggestion of doctors and treatment into serious action.

III

The waiting rooms of hospitals are somehow the worst place in the world next to the DMV. It seems like everyone is stuck behind a mountain of inescapable paperwork and legal noise that makes it impossible to see someone who can help you. The ticking of the clock on the wall seemed to bounce off every wall and chair as I shut my eyes and tried to focus.

Phones were ringing. People were talking. The sounds of life were coming in and out through the door. Despite all of this – the blind man's voice stayed prominent in my mind. I could hear his words so clearly. It had to be a fiction. There was no way any of that was real.

Since childhood, I had suffered visions and night terrors. I had always seen things and was prone to migraines and nosebleeds. My parents had shelled out the cash to send me to therapy, specialists, doctors, treatment centers, sleep centers. At the very end, all I could do was learn to mildly control it. Sometimes it would fade, and I'd be free of it for weeks, months on end, yet it always came screaming back.

I wasn't even sure why I was here now. It's not like they're going to tell me anything useful or that I haven't tried before. I could cry. The stress of this was finally getting me to snap. Maybe I was crazy. Maybe I should check myself into someplace. Have them keep me for seventy-two hours, then just play it up and hope they never let me out. Or I could kill myself. Just take a gun and end it. At this point, it wouldn't matter. I just want it to stop. I want the pain, the voices, the visions, the nosebleeds, the headaches – I want it all to stop. I don't deserve this. Maybe I will kill myself.

The voice of the nurse calling my name brought me out of my head as I opened my eyes and followed her into a room. She took my blood pressure and some simple tests. The doctor came in shortly after her. The same old questions and tests, sleeping pills and muscle relaxers with a half-sympathetic smile and back into the world I go.

Back to the brick walls of my loft. I threw myself down on the sofa and stared at the wall as the sun was setting. I knew it was out there. Mocking me. The tentacle thing. The thing was ringing the bell in my vision. I knew it was there just looking at me and savoring every moment of my torment.

Sarah stopped by, but I told her I wasn't feeling well, and I was going to turn in tonight – I had called into work, and since I was in the building and hardly took days off, I was placed "on call" in the event of an emergency. I laid in my bed and watched the sun fade fully. The last rays of light seemed like a bastion of hope that was leaving, and now, the night had set over the city. I closed my eyes and let sleep consume me.

At first, there was black. There was nothing. There was the void – and then I saw the true scope of things. This black void wasn't a void at all but a body, a writhing moving creation. It's huge globe-like eyes stared down at me – as I ran in horror, a sea of leeches swarmed me. As I cried out, they filled my mouth and nose. I began to drown in the bloodsuckers. As I crawled my way back to the surface and out of this muck, I was no longer in my bed. Nor in the city.

I stood on ashen ground under a pale moon. A bonfire was raging as five naked women danced around the flames, a witches sabbath, a black mass. Their bodies had tattoos of the creatures I saw entering the church. They let out savage howls and pained cries as they tossed strange items into the flames, offering these items to whatever dark brood they served. In that cold pale light only warmed by the bonfire, I heard a beckoning bell calling out to these witches, to these women of sin. The bell did ring across the moors, and into my soul, a fear did enter.

I was not one to gaze on this ritual, and the ringer of the bell knew it. Fateful reaper steals my soul, for I have seen the horrors or horror. My sanity was quaking as I tried to fight this dream, to cast these visions from my mind. I awoke in a cold, screaming fervor. To my complete terror, I saw my arms and chest drawn with the witches' symbols. My body became a temple for these ill-wrought creatures. I raced to my bathroom, yet with every step taken, I seemed to sink into the floor. I heard the cursed chattering of rat teeth bounce off the walls of my loft.

Had I finally lost my sense?

I stumbled into my restroom, foaming at the mouth. My nose was bleeding, and the reflection in the mirror was a horrid, pale image far from my own, a young man with a cut and slit face, deep scars and wild yet dead eyes staring at me as I shattered the mirror with my fist, and I reached for my pills that the doctor gave me. My hand stung from blood. As I knocked back two pills, I fell backwards into the cold bathtub.

I broke.

I began to cry loudly, head aching, stomach in knots, throwing up, bleeding nose and hearing the chattering and mocking laughs around me, the witch ink causing my skin to boil and bubble as I writhed in pain in the bathtub. I could only look up and cry out, for in hopes it would all end.

The last of my strength was used to shakily stand. The lipless flesh man stood in front of me, a priest of whatever the dog-faced humans were baying to. The flesh man placed its claw on my forehead as it drove its thumbs into my eyes.

Black and quiet now, silence and peace. Everything melts away to silence.

When I came to, I was far away from the horror of my loft. A small candle burned on the side of a table and gave off a soft light. He was watching me. The blind man. I was somehow back in that unholy city.

"Welcome back, Traveler. See you found your way here."

I sat up slowly and oddly enough felt a level of peace being around a somewhat friendly face.

"How…what happened?" I was shaken and couldn't – nay – didn't know what to ask.

"The flesh man brought you here. Left you at the step of my door."

"Why? What are those things? What is this place? I demand answers!" My voice was high and shaky. I was not in a place of strength, and the blind man knew it.

He wheezed with a laugh as he took out a pipe from his pocket. "This place is hard to explain, and I only know very little. There was once a blood king who lived in and by flesh. He indulged so much, and his sins were far and wide. The blood king was so full of fear of death, he placed a curse across this land – his blood would bring about an endless, beautiful yet tragic decay. All those who followed like him or who served against him would feel his pain or rewards."

I laid my head back on the pillow and began to cry. "Enough with the riddles, old man. Tell me the point."

The blind man took a long drag of his pipe and stared at me "We of the faithful blinded ourselves to rid ourselves of the visions and horrors that took over the city. Those who didn't became the filth you see wandering the city. Now you got a choice, Traveler."

I lifted my head slowly as I listened to him. He tossed me a knife with a tiny spoon like tip. I stared at it as he smoked his pipe. "Are you of the faith?"

I sat up and saw the marks gone from my arms. "Traveler, you seen too much. Purge your skin. Admit your sin."

I slid the tool away from me. "I'm not going to blind myself – that's insane."

The blind man sat smoking as he tilted his head. "Traveler, you admit that the things you've seen are the work of the unholy, the vile, the wicked and indulgent acts of those who lived a life of sin. And you would still not purge yourself? Admit that you have wronged?"

I stood up and steadied myself. "Look, I just want a normal life. I never asked for any of this. This is not what I wanted, needed or even thought of. You and this whole fucked up place can leave me alone. I just want a normal life with normal people"

The smoke from his pipe was thick and smelled of oak as he exiled a rather large smoke plume. I coughed and hacked as I felt my lungs burn. I woke up coughing in my bed. The morning sun was shining through my window. The mirror was fixed. The tattoos were gone. Everything seemed fine. I heard a knocking at my door. I quickly dressed to get the door. To my surprise, it was Sarah – holding coffee and cheesecake.

"Ethan, hey there." She smiled sweetly as I smiled back, lacking energy. "Hey, are you alright? You look pretty tried."

I couldn't hide it so I just admitted it. "I'm exhausted, Sarah."

She frowned before perking up. "I brought something to help fix that." She held up the coffee and cheesecake as I welcomed her in. We sat down and I laid my head back. "What's been going on, Ethan? I've heard a lot of stuff. People heard you crying, screaming. You went to the hospital…I'm worried."

I didn't have the energy to lie. "Sarah, my night terrors have been coming back in a big bad way. I think it got worse when I hit my head" I lightly touched the back of my head as I slumped further into my chair. "My sleep's been wrecked, and when I do sleep, I keep having the worst dreams."

Sarah was showing signs of relatable pity. We've all had bad nights of sleep before. As I spoke, I assume she thought back to years of her childhood when the offhand bad dream would rouse her from the safety of her bed and send her running into the safety of her parents' room. I knew the look in her eye, and I could even guess what she said as she said it. "Why not try sleeping pills?" I didn't want to be rude, so I worked my way through the answer with as much grace as I could.

"Sadly, this is a little more intense than basic medicine can handle. My doctor gave me some meds to try and cut back." I smiled weakly.

"Ethan, as your friend, I'm worried about you. Is there any way I can help?"

She ate a piece of cake slowly as I coolly ran a hand through my hair. "Sarah, you being here, bringing me coffee and cheesecake and having a breakfast buddy, that helps more than you know. It makes me feel normal." We smiled at each other; then I saw it. I saw the ring on her finger. I froze out of fear. What was happening to me? She saw my expression and paused.

"Ethan, what's wrong?"

My voice was strained as I began to speak. "Sarah, what is that ring?"

Sarah looked down to her pointer finger at the silver ring with the small symbol on the front. "It was my grandmother's, grandmother's. Repeat that a few times, and you'll get to the original owner. It's some old symbol for something. Why?"

"That symbol looks like one of the things I see in my dreams. It's a—"

As I began to speak, Sarah finished my sentence. "—witches' rune." I froze in awe. I began to sweat bullets of fear. "It means protection. I was never one for that superstition, but it's a family heirloom."

My throat was tight when she spoke. I felt dizzy. I tried to make sense of it. "Sarah, I have a headache. I need to lie down. I'm sorry. You have to go." I stood up and walked her to the door.

"Well…call if you need anything." We hugged as she left. I closed the door and began to cry. I popped open the bottle of pills from the doctor and took a handful. Throwing myself on the bed, I cried as I felt my head get light. The sun became a beautiful blood red shade. I watched my loft change shape. Then I saw him. He came in waves at first. He was blurry, until I could see him in all his details.

He was a massive hulk of muscle. The flesh goat man stood, towering over me, his jaundice eyes looking down at me as I felt a flutter of fear rush through my heart. The goat beast stomped his hoof against the hardwood and sniffed the air. I was still in my bed. I was still awake. My head felt fuzzy as the beast snarled. My heart was pounding in my chest, I couldn't breathe, and the goat seemed to smile as blood began to drip from my nose. The goat beast stuck out a long savage claw, and with its razor-sharp nail drew a symbol on my chest in blood. I screamed out in pain and suddenly went deaf. The witch symbol on my chest prevented me from hearing. I saw the goat throw its head back as I could see the laugh almost leave its body. Somewhere in the dark of my mind, the quiet was replaced, replaced by the sound of witch-chanting and singing. The tattoos returned as a black figure appeared in the corner of the room and started slowly walking toward me. I felt the hairs on the back of my neck rise slowly. I couldn't see his face as he was wearing a mask. He was the doctor, the plague doctor. He sat on my chest, and with a long medical blade, he drew the runes on my chest. I couldn't move nor cry out. Tears streamed down my face.

Suddenly, the dog-faced humans appeared and lit a fire as they started to praise the goat beast. The goat beast raised his arms to bask in the praise, and suddenly, I was lifted into the air by the hands of the mockery parade. My loft had been turned into a place of worship. I was placed on my knees, my hands were bound together, and I was forced to kneel. The dog-faced humans circled me as I tried to fight against this. Suddenly, I woke up in a cold sweat screaming. The dream had ended.

IV

I sat in my bed, the city outside the window asleep. The complex I was in, asleep. Quiet, peaceful and yet the storm raged inside my head. I stood up and walked to the mirror. My nose was bleeding heavily. I saw a distorted face in the mirror, and this time I stared it down. It stared back. I washed my face as the distorted face washed its face also. I had made my mind up – walking into the kitchen, I grabbed a knife and placed the blade on the stove. The blind man was right. This was no way to live.

I stared at the knife as the edge of the blade became black with a slight tinge of red. The smoke from the metal rose and dissipated through the kitchen. Grabbing the handle, I took a deep breath. I closed my eyes and put myself in a happy place as I felt the heat from the knife touch my eyelid. I froze and thought about how crazy this was. I suddenly drove the knife into my left eye socket, a quick stab. The heat searing my eye, I screamed as I dropped to the ground, the sound of metal clanking off the hardwood floor. I didn't feel blood – instead I felt an odd sort of release. I felt like a pressure had been released from me. I felt around for the knife as I closed my eyes and quickly jammed the blade into my other eye. I fell back on the floor, holding my hands to my face as I felt chains slide off me. I had been bound my whole life – now I was free.

I made my way back to my bed and laid down. I heard odd sounds but couldn't see. This was a trick of the mind. I fell into a black void of sleep.

Sarah discovered me the next morning along with Patrick and Rick. They found the knife, and I was rambling about chains. Apparently, the dog-faced humans had returned in the night and the walls and floor of my loft had been covered in strange symbols. I was taken away with a crying Sarah trying to hold my hand. I was moved to Pleasant Falls

Hospital. Here I sit and smile, facing what I believe to be the window. I know one night the blind man will come for me. I know one night they'll all come back for me. The doctors said I was suffering from an extreme case of encephalitis. They also claim the compound effect of night terrors and apparently, I had a high dosage of natural toxins normally found in plants. From the interviews I gave and the days leading up to the "Event," I had appeared to ingest a lot of it. When they went to interview Sarah and the others – Sarah was gone. All they found was a book of cooking recipes and various jars of plants from the night shade family.

It's time for sleep now though – maybe the blind man will come and take me. Maybe I won't wake up. I just know that for the first time in a long time, I can sleep. I can sleep.

San Tino 88

I

The house sat silent on a dark and quiet street. The street lights flickered as a soft breeze rushed through the neighborhoods. One house was more silent than the others. From outside, he snuck in. He walked through the house, carefully looking at the pictures on the wall. With every step up the stairs, he grew more excited. He found the girl asleep in her room. He quickly rushed in and covered her mouth with a rag. Come early morning, as the sun rose, the mother and father let out a petrified scream. Their little girl had vanished in the night, and all that was left in her place was a doll – a doll with its hair removed and replaced with patches from their daughter's hair.

The Doll Maker had struck again.

It was a long summer in San Tino. Along with people going missing left and right, the locals feared the "Doll Maker." He was the local boogeyman of the town. He had taken five children so far, all from their homes, from their beds, and in their places, he left dolls with one piece of the doll replaced by a piece of the child. Sometimes it was a finger. Sometimes it was hair. Sometimes it was the eyes or the heart. They say the heat makes people crazy. This was a particularly hot summer.

"Goddamnit, Karen! Do something!" Joel Bradman pleaded with San Tino's Sheriff.

"Joel, close the door, and don't ever speak to me that way again." Karen Pierce had been the sheriff in San Tino for a few years now. San Tino was a town that was no stranger to the violent and bizarre. Karen Pierce had grown up in the San Tino sun and sand. Her father was a policeman. When he was killed on the job, she had made it her life's work to follow in his footsteps and prevent other parents from leaving their children early – so far it was hard to tell who was winning that war.

Joel Bradman was one of the many parents who was spear-heading the civilian hunt for Doll Maker. His child was the first to go missing. Karen and Brad sat inside Karen's office as the rest of the station was blowing up with phone calls and faxes. Karen told Joel what she had told everyone else. "We've done background checks and interviews with all the toy makers and hobby shops within a thirty-mile radius. We have a list of possible suspects. Joel, I understand you and everyone else want answers. We're working, and if we're not working fast enough for you – then I am sorry. I know sorry won't bring Sam back. Sorry won't bring any of them back, but this is what we have to work with, and until we get more, we're doing the best we can."

Joel Bradman had heard her speak, and he sat in his anger and pain. "Karen, you don't have kids. You don't know what it's like."

This was a personal attack of sorts. San Tino among the locals was a tight community where gossip was passed and traded like baseball cards. Karen had a miscarriage last summer. It wasn't her first. Medically she was unable, and after a long and strained fight with her husband, Karen finally had to remove that ring from her finger. Hearing Joel say those words, she shot him daggers. Joel sank into the chair – he knew he crossed the line.

"You can leave now. I need to get back to work." Joel went to speak, but the damage had been done. He got up and left. Karen grabbed a bunch of files off her desk. She was going out on her second round of interviews. Sheriff Karen Pierce left the building and went to her truck. The morning droned on and on, more of the same thing. No-end leads and dead-end leads.

Karen knocked on yet another door. She was sweating. The early morning sun had given away to the midday heat. Karen looked up both sides of the street before the door swung open. "Ah, Good afternoon, Sheriff. How can I help?" Karen found herself staring at Philip Patterson. He was a toy crafter and hardware store owner. He had been helping with the recovered dolls.

"Phil, hey I have some more questions to ask." Karen held up a file and was welcomed in.

"Let me get you some water or lemonade. You look like you're melting." Philip returned to the living room and sat down across from Karen. He placed a glass of ice water in front of her as he himself drank a lemonade. "How can I help?"

Karen handed him the file. "More parts recovered. You were right. The dolls are made from composite parts. They're pieced together over weeks and months it would seem…which shows premeditation." Philip looked at the photos of the dolls as he slowly drank his lemonade. Karen took a long, nice sip from her water as she took off her hat and sat back. "What's worse Phil…the dolls are made to look like the kids."

Philip threw the file down and wiped his eyes for a moment. "That's sick Karen. How can I help?"

Karen took another drink from her water as she stood up. "I was wondering if you could tell me or walk me through how to make a doll. If any special parts or equipment was needed, we could call companies who've made any sales. I assume all the records are stored and stocked at some warehouse or company plant, right?"

Philip stood and waved Karen to follow him. "You're right. I can walk you through it and show you what parts and pieces you can ask about." Karen walked down the hallway as she had before. She had always admired Philip strength. His kid had drowned years ago, caught in a rip tide and taken down. They tried to revive her but to no avail. That's what got Philip into toy making. They walked out to Philip's workshop.

"Alright Karen, so that table over there has pretty much all the basic parts." Karen walked over to the table as Philip walked up next to her and held an instruction manual for a doll. "Most of it is a lot of small screws, washers, nothing overly special."

Karen and Philip spent the next half an hour going over the process and parts. Karen had a list of parts that would be the most likely to be ordered. "Thanks, Phil. This will be helpful."

Philip smiled as they shook hands and left the workshop. Karen reached the center of the hallway, before she felt it. Her head was slammed against the wall. Then she felt something tight and thin coil around her neck. "Karen, Karen, Karen. Shoulda left it alone." Karen was lifted to her feet, and Philip slammed her head against the table. She blacked out.

II

Karen came to, strapped into a chair with a blinding light shining in her face. She was dazed and confused. She went to speak, but Philip cut her off. "I've never made a mannequin before. You're going to be the first." Karen looked around her surroundings. She wasn't in the workshop. She saw doll parts scattered around the room, and then she saw it and screamed. "Oh, you saw my little pile, didn't you?" Philip stepped back so she could see it all. Skeletal remains in a pile on the floor. "You're in my secret workshop, Karen. Ya know, you got so close, but I couldn't have you getting smart. Don't worry. I moved your car off the street – not like anyone comes this far out anyway." He smirked as he sat down at a desk. "I've never worked on a long-term project Karen. This should be a challenge."

Karen tried to move her head slightly before she spoke "Why are you doing this?"

Philip turned to face her. "Karen, you of anyone should know how special children are. I mean, after you and Bob…well, what you went through isn't right. The loss of a child…it really puts things into perspective for you. Don't worry, Karen. We'll make the rest of your body like your womb, plastic. I'll even improve on mother nature and make it flawless. I'm choosing a child for you right now."

Philip wiped his eyes as he turned to her. "I'm sure you have a million questions. Let me explain to you, Karen. People age. People die. When I held my little girl after she was dead, it struck me that she would be young forever. She would never grow old, never know heartbreak, bills, stress, worry, actual pain. She will forever be a child – then I stopped feeling pain. If I could have a flawless forever child, why couldn't other people too?" Philip stood up and walked over to Karen as he held her chin. "You've already aged, but don't worry. Soon, you'll be the Madonna with Child."

Karen moved her chin as he let her go. "Phil, people will come looking for me. I'm law enforcement."

Philip leaned against the wall. "I'm sure they will, and when they do, they won't find a single trace of you. The car is out of sight, and no one knows this place exists. If I were you Karen, I'd get comfortable with the idea of being a mother after all. It's a process." Philip left the workshop and left Karen in the dark.

Hours went by and the sun dropped behind the San Tino horizon. The last golden rays of sun turned to an ebony shade that coated the city and beach. Philip had been going about his business all day, and now his darker activities were about to manifest again. Philip walked alongside the house and stared up at the window as the light shut off. He had been picking this girl out for weeks. Philip walked to the end of the street by his van and popped the back. Grabbing a few tools, he moved to the city gas line. Philip pried open the cover and attached a silver and green cylinder to the nozzle. He then looked at his watch and left the device. He knew the family would soon be out light a light. The sleeping gas would leave them out for hours with none the wiser.

Philip lockpicked the front door and walked into the house, wearing a small gasmask. He walked up the stairs and found the little girl passed out hard in her bed. He gently lifted her up and walked out of the front door with her. She was waking as Philip's van pulled up to his house. He placed a rag over her face, and she quickly succumbed to sleep.

Karen had spent the day taking stock of the room she was trapped in, looking for any avenue of escape, any way to free herself. Her wrists were raw and bleeding. She had been fighting all day against her restraints, and amazingly enough, she had made progress. Philip had made an oversight. He had never held a grown adult captive before, and therefore, the chair was easy enough to free. The police had already raided the house and freed Karen. Three armed officers were waiting in the house, and Karen was armed with a gun.

Philip opened his door and walked inside, holding the unconscious child in his arms. There was a heavy tension in the air. Unknown to Philip, he was about to be caught. All he needed to do was open the door and see Karen, place the child down and then the trap would spring. Philip opened the door to his workshop and placed the child down as he pulled back a rug, revealing a trapdoor to a sub-basement and his secret workshop. As Philip swung the door open and grabbed the girl, he entered his basement.

"Look, Karen. I brought you your child." Philip placed the girl down as he saw Karen's wounds. "Oh no." Philip walked over to her and began to inspect her wrists. "Karen, I know it's not ideal, but this is really uncalled for." He pointed to the girl. "You don't want to scare her, do you?" Philip stood up and walked over to his workshop bench. "Just think, Karen. Soon, you and your baby girl will be the eternal family, the Madonna and child, the loving mother and innocent lamb."

Karen tilted her head down and took a few moments to prepare herself. As Philip turned back to his work, he began to draw out plans for the Karen and the child. Suddenly, with all she had, Karen rushed Philip. The chair was still attached to her by the wrists, but she shouldered him and screamed. At that moment, two officers threw up the hatch lid and rushed down with guns out. Philip was overwhelmed and caught off guard. Before he knew what was happening, Philip was placed on his knees and his hands were cuffed.

San Tino could sleep easy. The girl was returned to her family. Philip was never heard from again – at least, not in San Tino. His transport truck was found on the side of the road with both drivers knocked out and no sign of Philip.

People always go missing in San Tino. That's no surprise. Maybe Philip was one of those people who got added to the missing person list. Maybe Philip broke out. The story is mostly urban legend now.

Pickman's Student

I

The final rays of sunlight faded as the sleepy small California town settled in for the night. One citizen rose to set about his work.

Walking from his bed into another room, he flicked on a light switch as the soft yellow glow lit the space. Vick Chambers exhaled slowly as he leaned against the wall of his studio and looked around, almost admiring his workshop.

Vick's studio was filled with paintings in various stages of completion. Sketches and drawings, full on canvas paintings littered the room, each with some horrorscape of hell. Vick felt safe among his demons. These devils of the pit, in a way, were his closest friends. Vick Chambers felt the call to art very early on. He went through a rough patch in high school and found he had a taste for the dark, the gothic and vile. Unlike your Hot Topic, black on black, gothic trend setter, Vick was something different altogether. He had a natural wonder about the dark world and all of its secrets.

From the Gothic art and paintings to buildings and settings, the world and time consumed his mind, so much so, that he soon began to express himself in the form of painting. Each year, his skills grew along with his knowledge of the dark and unspeakable eldritch horrors of old myth. From vampires and werewolves to changelings and squid-like gods of old, Vick had read and studied them all, every myth and lore and some old, long forgotten history. His skills in art quickly allowed him a ticket to Temple Art Academy at the age of nineteen. It was here that Vick's art was given a true validation. Before the art school, his high school teachers and peers were beginning to become repulsed by the art that Vick was displaying. His second term at Temple, Vick would find his muse, his guide and in his mind, his real teacher.

In an old monograph of weird art, Vick came across a name and a painting that would set the goal for him. Richard Upton Pickman. The piece selected was called *Ghoul Feeding* and showed in grotesque sharp features some kind of dog-faced humanoid gnawing on the remains of a human. The face and features of this creature captured Vick's eye, and the remainder of his time at Temple was used in tracking down any and every remaining trace of Richard Upton Pickman and his life story. By the time Vick Graduated, he was a well-known name in the art community. His pieces became much darker, sharper and all the more real.

Vick was a now a man in his mid-twenties, but was well regarded as a master of horror painting along with being an expert – one of the few – of Richard Upton Pickman. Vick had gathered quite an impressive collection of Pickman's work. Some pieces were bought, traded and stolen. He did whatever he could to collect and own a Pickman. While the world at large had all but forgotten the man, his name and work were well known to Vick, a well-known and widely rejected painter whose work boarded on the obscene. Witches and dog-faced humanoids, rat-like vermin overrunning the peaceful New England cities. Pickman went missing one night from his almost unknown studio he hired out under the name Peters. His body was never found, and throughout the years, his art was passed around in outsider art collections and galleries.

Vick had tracked down the studio, the names and collectors, the grandchildren of the one or two colleagues Pickman had, and even the remaining one or two art board members themselves who knew Pickman, Vick had traveled to Boston and tracked them down. He interviewed them, and as soon as he said the name, they shuttered at the memory. Vick had found the old studio – it had been torn down. Vick had traveled to Salem – where Pickman was from – and spoke to the family who lived in a house that once belonged to Pickman's father. Vick had traveled the subway systems and the tunnel system of Boston. He took notes and pictures, spent a summer and winter in Boston, the

North End where according to Pickman himself, is the place for an artist. Vick had returned home to California with a wealth of knowledge and actual work by the man. According to Vick, Pickman was his teacher, and he would carry on the work Pickman did.

Vick smiled as he lifted himself off the wall of his studio and walked toward the canvas in the middle of the room.

This particular piece was entitled *The Admirer*.

It was a ghastly piece. A woman stood changing in front of her window, and outside looking inward, hunched over and drooling, was a pale, narrow and gangly, filth creature. It had huge milky-white eyes and long, gaunt fingers as strings of sickly, yellow bile hung from its mouth.

Vick Chambers had truly become a student of Pickman, and while he carried on Pickman's work, he never once copied the man's style. Vick wanted to stand out, but one who knew Pickman's work would be able to tell where his style had changed and how.

Vick put on his headphones and began to work on the piece. The sun had long set by now, and the atmosphere inside the studio was thick.

Often times, Vick would let his mind wander, and he would wonder whatever happened to his satellite mentor. Vick believed as Pickman believed that there was something of the old world alive and well, if you knew where to look. The west coast didn't have any ghosts or demons. It was out of touch with the gods of old, and any trace of them had been so far publicized that they may as well have been billboards. Vick had traveled to the East Coast and New England in hopes of catching the ghosts and spirits that Pickman had spoken of – to no end, at least nothing more than myth, rumor and hushed whispers about local folklore. Whatever Pickman saw and knew, time and the modern world had killed it off. Vick had missed it by fifty years or so.

He had found copies and fakes of many old and ancient texts that he believed would help him see behind the veil as Pickman did. That includes but is not limited to *De Vermis Mysteriis*, *The Book of Azathoth*,

The Texts of Rile & Kaine, Occult and Obsidian, An Index of the Soul, and last but not least, that dreaded text – *The Necronomicon.* Vick had never taken any of these much further than research. However, he was well aware of the local East Coast myth and stories, the horror that befell Dunwich, that ill-fated and still unexplained trip to the Antarctic. Vick had visited Miskatonic University and the now sister university Shade-Hill.

If it even remotely involved Richard Upton Pickman, Vick had been there, found, documented and researched it thoroughly. The world was just not the same though, and Vick knew it. There was something about man, about humanity, about progress that pushed the old world out and stamped it into history, then rumor, then myth and then ghost stories to be told around campfires. Vick had been painting for three hours when he stopped and took a step back. A hunger had come over him, and as he blinked for the first time since he started painting, his eyes suddenly stung a bit. "Better take a break." He placed his paint and brush down as he retired to the kitchen. Vick grabbed sandwich material from the fridge and quickly made himself a snack. Sitting down, he looked out of his kitchen window and saw pitch black, the ebony scene of a cold California night. He wished for a touch of the old, that haunted and horrid, magical and fiendish world that the texts he read spoke of, when the old ones would wake, when long forgotten cyclopean sunken cities would rise from murky depths and the old world would show this new pink and clean world just what life, death, fear and living really was.

II

Days had past, and Vick Chambers returned home after a short gallery opening. To his amusement, he had gathered a fair share of shocked and horrified faces at his newest pieces. He was regarded in the art community as "A painter of the inescapable horror that Dante wrote." This, of course, was taken as a title of pride for Vick. He had delivered a talk on art and painting theory about how if you really want to paint, you need to add blood into the canvas. Get some dirt, mud, blood, spit and semen into the paint. Forget elbow grease. Cut a vein and stable it to the canvas. The more of yourself that is in the art, the better the art is. Vick had hours upon hours of art talk and theory, theory of the soul and what it means to be human. He would and could sit for ages to discuss these topics.

Vick Chambers believed that art was the one and only true expression of the soul. He believed it to be the world's real gift. He had seen countless, soulless pieces by halfcocked doodlers, believing themselves to be introspective and reflective. This type of soulless art disgusted him, disgusted him to the point where he believed he should punish the eyes of the world by creating art that was designed to assault the senses. Vick was starting a new piece, his most ambitious and vile yet.

That's when he saw it. He had almost forgot about it. In his bag, the gift had been given by a fan and fellow artist of the macabre. They had a discussion about the morbidity in life and how best to represent it through art. She handed him a book, one she said changed her life.

Vick went to his bag and pulled out the old tome. It was a rufous leather that looked well worn. The pages felt old and were well used. This vile volume was in surprisingly good condition for being clearly of older times.

The sun had set, and instead of his art tonight, Vick would read through this arcane text and see exactly what – if anything – he could gleam from its infernal pages.

The first page of the book brought Vick's eye and mind to a complete freeze. He saw the title of the book, and an uncontrollable smile crossed his face. Vick was now the owner of the rare *Science of the Gate and Seals*, a book believed to have the power to open gates and portals to other realms and worlds and also summon things from beyond, whatever feverish nightmare hellscape anyone could fathom.

The book was said to have come from Salem stock, a sort of collective journal from the original Salem witches and their kin who had narrowly escaped the likes of Cotton and Increase Mather and the Hales. Throughout the decades, the book was said to have passed from witch cult to witch cult, collecting only the most tried and true spells and incantations. There was only ever one copy to keep it truly secret and to make sure that no novice or layman would dabble in matters far beyond their scope. Vick was no practitioner of magic, yet he had done his fair share of reading among those books that said how to contain powers of an otherworldly sort, and he knew enough to know that *if* he were to attempt any kind of wizardry, the steps involved would require a savage and most illegal shopping list. Vick turned these ideas into subjects for new paintings in his new collection.

"It's what Pickman would've done," he said to himself in a self-assured tone. The night droned on, and with each page of unspeakable horror, Vick felt somehow "closer" to Pickman and his art. It was as if this book was a sort of direct link to the man and that erroneous world. Vick carefully inspected every page, every detail of the drawings inside, every word and step – of course, he would never try and use any of this. The idea of trying magic or any kind of otherworld craft seemed like a faraway idea to him. He was a man, born of man. He had a mother and father. He was born into a world that was far removed from ghosts, ghouls, demons, devils, gods and superstition altogether. This was twenty-twenty-three, after all. Surely the idea of witchcraft and conjuration had been so far removed that any actual danger was easily bypassed. It was now only in the movies and video games that belonged to the mainstream world. As Vick thought about this, he turned a page and felt a sting against his index finger. The drag of the edge of paper sliced into his skin. He recoiled quickly as he looked at the paper cut. He quickly sucked on his finger for a moment, before he closed the book and walked into his art studio, letting the blood on his fingertip pool. He slid it down the side of his new painting and smiled at himself.

Over the passing weeks, Vick's new collection took horrifying turns and twists. Also, his dreams became more graphic and vivid. Sleep became less about resting and more about entering that bleak void. First, it looked like a fog, then a haze, then a red ashen sky with bone dry gravel. Beyond this space, Vick had seen the heavens part and the black universal galaxies crash into one another. He had seen a solar system swallowed whole by some shadowy colossal being.

Vick had dreamt once of a young woman. She was naked and dancing with a goat mask on her head. As she spit red liquid over a bonfire, she was joined by several other naked women of varying ages, all with the heads of animals. Their nude bodies had blood drawings on them, old symbols and scenes depicting sacrifice. Surely these were the sinister and ancient rituals of old, not of the devil but of the gods of old, from the first and second ice age, the sleeping gods who could swallow the universe and blanket the stars in pitch obsidian.

It was no wonder when Vick awoke in a cold sweat, how he would rush to his paint room and work like a mad man. He would spend fifteen, sixteen, twenty hours a day purging his mind of these horrors and committing them to canvas. Right next to his canvas, at all times, sat *Science of the Gate and Seals*. He would use it as reference, although he had come to learn that the book itself had oddly rigid paper. He had cut himself on the edges or sides more than ten times. So much so, that some pages had drips and small streaks of blood on them. The sleep deprived artist rarely ate, and when he did, it was always in a hurry, something fast and quick to make so that he could return to his work.

One time, Vick thought his mind was playing tricks on him as he could've sworn that he saw one of the pictures in the book move. He thought he saw a snake-headed woman bow to a five-pointed star monolith. Vick rubbed his eyes with one hand, and as he went to close the book, he cut his finger again. The sting didn't bother him anymore. The work he was producing was of a high and dark quality, the likes he had always hoped of.

Vick walked into his bathroom and looked out of the fog-styled window. It was night. When was the last time he had seen the sun? He couldn't remember and didn't really mind. As he turned on the hot water, Vick stripped down and stepped inside his shower-bathtub combination. He sat down and closed his eyes as the hot water ran over his body. He felt dirt and grime slide off and down the drain as he just listened to the sound of the water hitting the bathtub. He must have drifted off, because suddenly Vick heard a noise inside the bathroom with him, and as he opened his eyes, he saw her.

A woman standing before him. She was naked save for a brown cloak. Her skin was pale, and her face was hidden by the hood. Vick just sat under the hot water and looked at her. She spoke in a dreamlike voice, yet the words she said were far from picturesque.

"Sleeping dreamer, eye of Leythis, waking world and blood. So do the old ones stir, and so shall you find them where you sleep, in mind's eye and prison hold for shaking and breaking chains of old rattle against the walls."

Vick had no time to ponder this as she lifted the cloak to reveal a dog-faced humanoid. It looked like a gargoyle from some centuries-old church. Vick felt a rush of fear, and as he screamed, he woke in his shower. Vick franticly looked around his empty bathroom. He stood up and shut the water off. He dried off and walked to his room where he lay down and closed his eyes. Maybe now, he could afford a day or two from his art. He had been working and reading hard, but even the most dedicated artist needed a break, a time to recharge and collect themselves.

III

A red ashen sky stretched across overhead – before him – an old twisted and haunted city. Wood and stone buildings that towered and teetered into the crimson abyss surrounded him. Vick rose to his feet, and he tasted the harsh thick air. Every breath he felt as if he had to cough. Torches acted as the city lighting system. However, these were not normal wood and cloth. They were large, inhuman devices. The head of the torch seemed to be bits and pieces of human flesh, while the rest of the stalk were bone. Vick looked slowly around at this vile city as words and sounds failed to leave his mouth.

Suddenly, from out of the dark, somewhere not in eyesight, the ringing of a bell was heard. A large droning tone that seemed to shake the very ground. Slowly, the doors of the buildings were opening. From under the city – sewer gates and from out of the shadows – as if called by that bell, the city population moved onward.

Vick saw before him a mass of true horrors.

These things were reflections of the very pit. Some where the known dog-faced humans, the animal-headed human kin, the slimy, the winged, the scaled, the vile, bile and putrid.

Vick quickly searched his pockets for pen and paper, anything to jot down whatever he could see. From the front of the mass, a sudden bonfire was lit, and infernal chants started to thunder from inside the crowd.

"Hail the butcher. Hail the fallen true lord. Deny your gods and cast off sin as your true self, for we are aspects of the goat. We are but pieces of the void, and together we shall be whole. Purge the innocent, for their sins are deliberate, are of the butcher, as animals, so we are as animals, so we shall be, and in the coming age, let the rats gnaw on the bones of the interlopers."

Vick heard these words being yelled by some cloaked woman standing near the fire. She had both hands outstretched, and although Vick could not place her, he somehow knew she was the high priestess of Babylon. She was the plague bearer, the rat woman, the healing hand and death touch, the messenger and envoy. She was the voice of some goat-headed blood and war god who had birthed, lived, been worshipped, died, resurrected, been forgotten about, and now waited silently in some pit thousands of years before the modern gods would come to hold America's heart.

Vick Chambers awoke on his floor next to his paintings, and the book was next to him. Putting every thought aside, Vick went to work, and he created a new painting, a black sabbath, a gathering of animal-headed witches.

The following weeks had come and went, and Vick Chambers now sat sleep deprived, hungry, unwashed and feeling far more at peace than ever before. His art studio had now seven full and finished paintings. All were vile images of unspeakable horrors. He sat in a chair and admired his work, feeling drained of self and soul, giving away so much of himself to the art. This was the point.

Vick had taken every nightmare, every hellscape, every ounce of the void and painstakingly recreated it on canvas. During this time, Vick had turned his attention to a new idea. Victor Chambers had taken his blood and made a sort of blood serum. He mixed it into his paints thus literally putting himself in the work. The man, the work, the horror, the mortality was now one. Vick stood shakily and walked to his bathroom. He flicked on the light and hot water. He sat down in the bathtub and closed his eyes.

Victory pulsed through him. On some endless unseen high and satisfaction, Vick Chambers felt like he had won. He had put himself through the worst of hell, the darkest side of mankind, the true war of the soul. He had grabbed as much of that twisted void as he could and dragged it into the light, kicking and screaming, and now he could rest.

The sense of peace, of togetherness, the sense of purpose settled his mind. His anxiety and fear washed away as he rested and let the water rinse off his grime. If man was meant to exist, Vick had reached further than any living or dead human ever had. He had seen what Pickman saw. He had touched the void, and in dream or not, in waking life or not, in hell or not, in some fever of a paranoid dreamer or not, Vick had been there – and he came back.

He had won. He had reached a tall and isolated but beautiful peak. He had crested over black waves of time. The answers to man's deepest questions of soul, life and death, not only had he answered, but he had painted. This was victory. This was purpose. His mind eased. His body relaxed. The papercuts on his finger from the old book seemed to be sore, but that didn't matter now. The work was far from over, but he had nothing left at the moment. He had to let the well of creativity build back. He had to rediscover inspiration. He had to take a break. He would release these seven and call his agent. He was going to take a small vacation, at least, to purge himself and get a clean slate.

Suddenly, a thought entered his mind, a thought that caused an assholic and knowing smirk to cross his face. "Ni dieu ni maître." Vick knew he was using the term out of context, but he felt the idea of the message was the same. He had suddenly surpassed Richard Upton Pickman in every way. Somehow, someway, Vick had found the old world in full. He had found the darkest void Pickman could only dream of but never pull into light. Vick had traveled far beyond his former mentor. He was now once again without a master, without a teacher, without a mentor, and he was once again free to break himself and cast himself new. Vick was ready for the next stage of his art.

However, as he sat thinking this, as he sat pondering this, he thought he heard something, something coming from his studio.

He stood up and shut the water off. Hearing the sounds of footsteps and shifting paintings, Vick walked toward the bathroom door, and from under the door, a trail of red paint crept forward. He threw the bathroom door open and rushed to his workplace.

There in the rearranged workspace was a figure hunched over. Paint cans were spilled over the floor, and a lot of the work had been painted over with globs and marks. A rage filled Vick's heart. A fire of hell took residence inside him. Vick took a strong step forward and spun the figure around. He was too angry to be scared as he threw a fist into the thing's face.

Vick began a wild assault on this creature, the stomach, the face. Vick struck it hard several times, each with a stronger blow than the last, the fire raging inside him. In the commotion, a can of paint thinner was knocked over, and Vick cast the thing down to the floor. It choked out blood and gurgled. It was a dog-faced thing, some pale, leather skinned dog-faced humanoid. Vick slammed it against a wall and looked at his defaced paintings. He then looked down at the creature and mounted it. Wrapping both hands around its throat, Vick began to choke the life out of it, his fingers feeling the old hard leathery skin. The thing started to laugh as it tossed Vick off it and stood up. Vick froze as the thing held up an oil lamp over the paint thinner that had pooled on the floor. Their eyes met, Vick's mortal eyes and the dog-faced drooping wild white orbs.

It was now that Vick could take in the figure in all its savage mockery of physical form, the bulk of loose leathery skin, a stench of fetid air. Anger and fear flooded Vick's mind. A stringy yellow glob of spit hung from its mouth. It had huge loose lips that showed off a gnarled, jagged and ruined set of human-like teeth. Some were jagged points. Others were short and squared off. It shook the oil lamp as if to taunt Vick.

The ringing of a bell suddenly caught both off-guard. The dog-faced thing put the oil lamp down and walked past Vick, almost as if under a trance. Vick's anger raged, but the sound of the bell seemed to hold back the rage as he followed the dog-thing.

Through the front door, Vick found himself staring at that crimson ashen world, the huge twisted towers with those vile flesh torches. A mass of cephalopod humankind droning toward that bell. A huge bonfire was lit by cloaked figures outside of a massive grim looking church. Vick hurried to an alley where he could watch without being seen.

The town square was now a mass of chanting and bubbling sounds from lipless and quivering tentacled and beaked mouths. Some had wolf-like snouts or cockroach-like bodies. A large cross was lifted into and placed down in front of the bonfire. A young girl with a painted symbol of a snake on her exposed body was nailed in place. She screamed loud; fear was echoing through every cry. She cried out for someone to help her. To try and save her. From atop the church, something scaled down to the cross and placed an oversized claw on her lips as if to silence her.

It was a sort of chimera. The legs were that of a goat. The body was of a female, yet it had 6 dried and crusted udders as if overfeeding led to them being sagging flesh bags. The arms were that of a man; however, each one had slithering-like snake veins that snakelike heads would poke out at random times from quarter-sized pores. The hands were that of a mole with long jaundice claws. The neck and head belonged to a mammoth of a python. To the trained eye, it was a Titanoboa. Its long, forked tongue slid out and licked the young girl from foot to hair. From the back of this void-spawn arched two large angel like wings. It grabbed the cross and hissed loudly as the mass of minor horrors seemed to exalt excitement. The obsidian seraphim held the cross over the bonfire as the screams of the girl were cut short. The fires grew higher as the snake thing held its head to the sky and let out a noise of hell static.

Vick held his mouth shut. This entire scene was too much. He had crossed over into waking life. This couldn't be a nightmare. It felt too visceral. Stammering back, Vick ran into a large pigman in a leather apron. Its sweaty skin slid against Vick's, and he let out a scream. The pig looked down and let out a series of low and husky grunting. Vick, without thinking, ran into the street and was seen by a cluster of small rat-faced children who squeaked and chattered loudly as they saw him. At the same time, sitting atop the torches were these even smaller batlike toddlers. Their shrill voices caught the attention of the crowd at the bonfire as the air filled with the shrill siren of these daemonic imps.

The snake-headed seraphim snapped its head toward the commotion, and with a commanding hiss, the crowd seemed to gain their own senses back, now all turning and charging toward Vick who was running down the gnarled and twisted cobblestone. His heartbeat was in his ears, and he ran like the wind, as from behind him, a cacophony of infernal fiends surged at his back, snarling, nipping, biting, clawing, hissing, squeaking, chattering, all manner of animal humanoid devolution that reflected the grotesqueness and inhuman mockery of the pit when it looks back on the mortal coil.

Vick ran through crooked, narrow alleyways filled with old black brick and towering spire buildings. With every passing street, the city seemed to swell with hunger, another sacrifice for the old ones, the forgotten sleeping gods of the first stellar ice age, the ones Vick had read about in the book. Frozen and still, everlasting and sleeping in the far reaches of black outer space in between realms where fire becomes water and water becomes blood, where the air itself is toxic and the trees are of bone and ash, in cemetery star systems, the hibernating zodiac long forgotten by our modern world sleep and dream of their awakening. Vick was to be an offering to these primordial bodies.

Running to a section of town that broke away from the buildings, Vick crossed an old stone bridge that crossed a span of blackness. As Vick ran across the bridge, it collapsed and left an uncrossable gap save for the winged spawn. As the snake chimera hissed, the winged things flew after Vick as the land-horde began to backtrack and seek another way. Vick kept running, hearing the flutter of wings behind him when up ahead, he saw a row of trees and a swamp. Entering the mire, Vick fell directly into inky, black ice-cold sludge.

Then there was quiet.

Weightless and freezing, Vick could hardly feel the odd vines that slowly constricted his arms. He opened his eyes to see nothing, just void. Not knowing which direction was up, something inside him told him that that slight tug on his body was not just the mud and sludge he was stuck in, so the opposite direction of the tug was the way he needed to go. With the rest of his energy he pulled, arms and legs kicking. Every movement felt like a hundred pounds. His head throbbed. His lungs ached. Finally, something gave way, and he spat out muck as he took a lungful of air. Clawing his way to the mud, the raw odor of rotten seafood filled his nose, and he doubled over vomiting. Victor Chambers passed out in the mud of the wretched swamp.

IV

Suddenly, violently, Vick erupted from his bathtub, thoroughly drenched to the bone as the water from the shower head ran down and over the now overflowing bathtub. Sputtering and confused, half-drowned, he slipped onto his tile floor and was back in his quiet apartment.

There, on the cold tile, Vick threw up what looked like sewer water. Slowly standing and grabbing the sink to steady himself, Vick gawked at his washed-out appearance in the mirror. Running a hand through his hair, he reached over and shut the water off and allowed the tub to drain.

Time had passed, but he was unsure of how much.

How had he gotten home?

The rest of his studio sat in silence as what looked like sunlight poured through his window. Finally, catching his breath, he shakily walked to his front door and wrenched it open, allowing the fresh air and early morning sun to burst into his home.

Had this gone too far? Had his own mind begun to collapse under his lifestyle? Was the art and the walking in Pickman's shoes too much for him? Was this what happened to Pickman, he wondered?

For the first time in a long time, Vick Chambers sat down in the grass outside his studio and thought about life, a life away from the paint and canvas, a life away from the muck and mire and most of all, a life away from his satellite mentor Richard Upton Pickman.

Feeling the cool grass on his hands and the back of his neck, Vick closed his eyes and let the sun soak his skin, anything to wipe away that horrid chill from that inky black hellscape mire that infected his thoughts.

Here was a crossroads. Here was a measure of man, a measure of human endurance.

Anyone could and should and would have walked away, taken another route. The easy way out of something was to just walk away from it. Vick could just change his medium, change his style. He could give up his title as the enfant terrible of the art world. But wasn't this what he wanted?

The sun warmed his skin and with this grasp on reality, Vick doubled down on his conviction. He asked to see what Pickman saw. He wanted to know hell and the void. Vick wanted to master the abyss, at least on canvas. If this was his price to pay for the void, then so be it. Most of us never knew hell, and if Pickman was ostracized from the art world for what he saw, then good. At least he had conviction in his world view, and so did Vick.

Sitting up, he wiped his eyes and stood up. Taking a lungful of air and heading back into his studio, he closed the door and began a new work. For the next several weeks, Vick Chambers would be letting his canvas and his audience know what price he had paid.

Hours turned to days and days turned to weeks, weeks to months, and then one day, roughly seven months after Vick Chambers had lived hell, his studio door flung open. There, in the doorway, beer bottle in his hand, unwashed hair, and looking exhausted stood the artist in gutter glory. Reaching into his pocket, he pulled his cell out and made several texts to his would-be waiting agent and marketing team. Vick walked back inside his hobble and went to wash away the musk of the art. Within the Month, Vick Chambers stood at a front lobby desk, making idle chit chat as the doors to the gallery opened and a steady stream of art patrons, artists and fans found their way to the newest exhibit by the tortured genius of Vick Chambers. He titled this exhibit "Hell to Pay." As the night went on, people were as to be expected – horrified, offended and disgusted with the ugly and vulgar paintings they saw.

Vick smiled to himself as he left early. Sneaking out the back door and hopping into a car, he drove on the dark roads back to his home. The car came to a stop as Vick stepped out and froze at the sight of his door.

Kicked in.

Hurrying to the back of his car, he popped the trunk and grabbed a tire iron before walking toward his home. As he stood in the doorway and looked around, his eye was drawn to the closed bathroom door and the light leaking out from under the doorway.

"Hey fucker. I'm armed. Come out slowly." Vick raised the tire iron as he took a step into the darkened studio. He heard a noise from the side but was too slow as he was knocked to the ground. The tire iron was kicked away as Vick stood up in the moonlight. He saw a dog-faced horror, drooling globs of milky-white slime from its mouth. The horror lurched at Vick who ducked into the studio and rushed to the bathroom. As he threw the door open, the flames rocketed into the room. Heavy black smoke started to fill the room. As Vick was caught hacking and coughing, the heat from the fire started to climb up his body.

The dog-faced creature let out a sickening howl as the flames enveloped the room. The oil and paint thinner helped quicken the flames.

In the early morning sun, a crowd had gathered around the now smoldering remains of the studio. The fire fighters removed charred wood and paintings into a trash truck as no signs of life were seen. As Vick Chamber's manager and agent stood by looking, waiting for anything to salvage as the final payoff of their troubled and young cash-cow, they were handed a single painting, seemingly untouched by the fire.

The painting was a dog-faced creature standing in the middle of a church filled with paintings in various states of disrepair and completion.

Sprawled across the bottom of the piece in red paint was a name, signed.

R. Pickman

The Return of the Monkey's Paw

The quiet night air and stillness was broken by the sound of a single engine plane sputtering on the private runway. As the plane came to a rough halt, the man inside snapped out of his trance as he shook hands with the captain and walked down the short staircase onto the tarmac.

He quickly looked around as an average looking car pulled up alongside him. The driver of the car stepped out and hurriedly scurried around to the waiting man as he opened the back seat passenger side door. "Mr. Valentine." The driver slightly bowed his head as the man nodded and took his seat. It was then when he was comfortably in the car that he placed the leather and hardwood box next to him. He cradled it with one hand and couldn't help but smile. Leeland Valentine had spent decades searching, chasing rumor and myth, reciting legend and following footsteps – to the wilds of Borneo, the chapels of Spain, Italy and Romania, the Amazon, the mysticism of Morocco, Mexico and finally Iraq, Syria, Iran, Persia, and now back to the United States.

His fingers drummed off the box as he looked at it with the love of a father at his new born heir.

The car drove off the private runway into country road darkness. Leeland closed his eyes. At least, he was home. He had his prize, and soon his pilgrimage would be complete.

The wine slid off her breasts in the most pornographic way they could. She giggled as he licked at her pert nipples. He did another line of cocaine off her lower back and then stood up. This was William Hurstle, a man who got too lucky for his own good.

William came from a broken home on a broken street with broken dreams. He had dropped out of high school, been to jail for petty theft and minor drug charges, and then turned his life around.

William had failed upwards. While in jail, he had found himself talking to a confused but reasonable older man who spoke of the soul. He had spoken of the ways of the Lord. William, at first, disregarded all of this as nonsense, but then one day, the confused man showed William the light. A fortune could be made. Doors would fly open. Women, money, power, influence – it could all be easily attainable as long as you had faith.

William Hurstle converted his life in the public image and was released from jail. He was smarter. He started posting videos on YouTube about the Lord and the light, about the grace of God, and soon William was able to sign autographs when he walked out of his apartment.

Now here he was, the face of The First Order: His Grace, Our Savior.

On the surface, they were another peace and herbal cult who worked like a pyramid scheme. On a deeper level, they were true fanatics, searching for a way to control all faith and bring about a world religion through their eyes.

The girl who now laid on her stomach looked up to William, her eyes shimmering from the chemical cocktail they had both taken. She was 17, a runaway who found solace in the church and a home in his bed.

William was on the younger side of his thirties, good body, sob story, charismatic, charming and clever enough that even if anyone did find out about his active vices, he could spin a tale and convince them it was the way of the Lord. Yes, William Hurstle had truly failed upward into the best place he could be.

As he took a long drag from a cigarette, he looked at his naked reflection in the mirror and flexed.

That's when the door burst open. William panicked along with the girl as Leeland Valentine barged in. He took a moment to look around the room before showing visible disgust. He looked at the girl naked on the bed before marching over and grabbing her by the arm. She tried to fight as Leeland dragged her form the room and tossed her to his security team in the main lobby of the mansion. "Deal with her," he snarled. The spun girl sniffled, before the door slammed shut, and Leeland coolly ran a hand through his hair. William had now put on pants and was somewhat cowered.

"You immature ass," Leeland barked. "You'd risk everything I worked for – I gave you! You built, because I built it first. You'd risk your public image on a woman!"

William stood up and got a glass of water. "She won't tell. She loves me. I'm her savior," he quipped as he took a sip of water from an ornate glass.

At lightning pace, Leeland rushed to William and slapped the glass from his hand and grabbed the younger man by the throat. "Listen here, you piss-ant. I built you from shit. I built all of this from thin air. I was gifted and shown the way long ago. You are merely the puppet of the puppeteer, and I am merely the string that pulls you. Do *not* think yourself greater than you are, because I swear William, I *swear* I can and will rip the heart out of you and surrender it to our Lord, and I will be rewarded. Do you hear me you mentally defunct mutant?" Leeland pushed back William as he released him.

William had overplayed his hand, and he knew it. He may have been able to get away with that kind of smart talking bravado with his community or in his congregation, but when it came to Leeland, there was no room to give. William adjusted himself and took a knee in front of Leeland. "I'm sorry. You're right, Father."

Leeland softened as he put a hand on his shoulder. "Come, my son. You'll have to repent later. Now, you must gather the most faithful. Announce the time has come and a retreat for the most convicted of members of the order."

William raised his head. "You've found it?" His voice was full of hope and delight.

"I did," Leeland said. "It's in the car in its carrier box and in pristine condition. Now all we need is faith William. Faith and the Lord will provide."

"May the Lord be praised." whispered William as he went into prayer and closed his eyes.

Leeland outstretched his arms and closed his eyes as he tilted his head upwards. "Praise be to him."

A knock on the door made both men turn their heads as it opened slightly. A mountain of a man poked his head in the door. "Sirs, excuse the intrusion, but it's getting late and you said you wanted me to alert you to the hour of 2 am."

"Yes Jim, thank you," Leeland said and waved the guard away. Turning to William, Leeland adjusted his coat. "Get packed for a long weekend, and tomorrow at service, let everyone know. I'll be going on ahead tonight in order to prepare things for the upcoming event." William stood and both shook hands.

"Thank you for this opportunity, Leeland. It means the world."

Leeland stopped him short as he held a hand. "Don't thank me. Thank him." Leeland glanced up and then excused himself as he left the room. Back through the lobby mansion and now with his security in tow, one man opened the door and the other took the driver's seat. "Where's the girl?"

"In the trunk, Mr. Valentine," said the guard next to him.

"Good" replied Leeland "We'll dump her in the river along the road. She's another dead runaway the papers will love to write about."

In the days that followed, William and Leeland both set about to their respective work.

William was the face of the order, the salesman and leader, while behind the scenes and really running the show sat Leeland. The hushed rumor was that William was the adopted son of Leeland. This rumor, of course, was created by Leeland, and he let it spread organically. William was well-aware of it, and so he accepted the myth along with all the perks it brought with it.

The only real connection Leeland and William had was their connection to the order. Leeland had spent every waking moment of his existence in some kind of faith. He was brought up in Holy Mother Church. From there, he found his way into Catholicism. Any kind of Paganism or polytheistic faith made his blood boil. In truth, Leeland, at his core, loved God. He believed in God, and everything he did, he believed was in his service to, for and a showcase to God.

Leeland had gone so far down the rabbit hole of faith that he had gotten lost somewhere along the way, and in that isolated spiritual space, Leeland heard a voice, the voice of God. It gave him a mission, a quest. The voice told him to seek the ultimate moment and cry in the face of God.

Leeland then set out to the world. He spoke with shaman, priests, bishops. He did everything in his power to find relics and artifacts that he believed would bring him closer to God.

He needed money, more money than he had, and so he set out with a very specific idea – start a church of likeminded individuals who would pool their money and influence together and allow Leeland to operate as he needed, and he would bring them all the truth they all so desperately needed, and so The First Order: His Grace, Our Savior was born.

William had a growing following, and when Leeland heard about William, he made a phone call. William couldn't turn down the money, fame or influence that he would and could gain so much faster than what he was doing now. This was a no brainer.

They had churches all over the world, all manner of people, colors and creeds, and only a handful of the most trusted and most devout followers knew of Leeland and knew the actual purpose of the First Order.

Leeland had spent the better part of his life tracking down anything and everything that could provide him with his guiding light, to weep in the beauty and face of God, and after what seemed like a lifetime of relic hunting, he came across a hushed rumor and a dark tale that, maybe if handled correctly, could be the exact thing he was looking for.

Leeland had traveled ahead to the worship camp to ready things, and next to him in a very ornate wood and leather box sat the very item he had literally killed for.

He carefully opened the box and reached in as he pulled out a mummified but perfectly preserved monkey's paw.

The rumor was that this item was blessed by a fakir sometime hundreds of years ago. It was all about how fate can't be changed, and the laws of the world are in fact the laws of God so tampering with them would bring about a most undesirable outcome.

Leeland finally had it. The paw was passed along from person to person and family to family, and all who wished on the paw came to some grisly end. The paw was said to have the power to grant three wishes. It would be used and then seemingly vanish only to reappear elsewhere in history. It was sold, lost, buried. People tried to destroy it, but no amount of tampering could stop this holy and powerful relic from the world of men.

When he had finally acquired the paw, he tried to wish there on the spot but nothing happened. Leeland believed that after all that use, all that time being taken advantage of, it had somehow drained the paw of its blessing, and so Leeland determined that *if* a supreme act of honest faith was shown to the paw, it would and could be given its power back.

Leeland carefully put the paw back in its box for now and pulled a leatherbound notebook out from his briefcase. He began thumbing through it.

Names and numbers, dates and times. This notebook was Leeland's secrets of the stars. He had information on some very high-profile members of his church and dirt on others. Soon, he would call the chickens home to roost as it were. The man behind the money that allowed Leeland to operate in the first place had been waiting – some would say beyond patiently. Word had begun to make its way through proper channels that the time was at hand. Leeland was home and with the prize he so often obsessed over.

From car to plane to car again, Leeland finally stepped out in front of a big iron gate that two men unlocked and opened for him.

This was Fairaway Camp, the worship camp and retreat for The First Order: His Lord, Our Savior.

Although all were welcome, only a very select few were aware of the darker intent that was the real purpose.

Fairaway camp sits in the middle of the pacific northwest tucked away in the dark cold woods, surrounded by towering trees and bushes like a wall of greenery. Inside the area is a carved-out camp with wooden cabins, a lake, and several buildings that act as a workshop, a church, a cafeteria, and men, women and children centers for prayer and community.

Leeland stepped onto his self-anointed holy ground and looked up to the sky before clasping his hands together and turning to his men. "Let's not waste any more time."

The men closed and locked the gate as Leeland was handed a black portfolio.

William walked onstage as the church band finished their third song. He was wearing a white suit coat with tan pants and holding a bible. He smiled and waved out to the crowd.

"Hello and good morning, friends. Wasn't that music just awesome? I tell ya, these guys are blessed with the spirit and the Lord said and now you can blow the roof off this place." He waved to the crowd before making a gesture to quiet them down.

"Now today, I want to talk about our connections with God – how and when he speaks to us and how and when we know what to do. The Lord doesn't always use a clear voice. Sometimes he likes us to use our God-given intelligence to figure out his wants for us, and so we may help him by helping ourselves." William looked out to his congregation; he saw their eyes locked onto him. They hung on his every word as if he held the key to their salvation. William smirked to himself before starting again.

He made his sermon, and at the end of the hour and a half, he took a moment to remind everyone about the prayer weekend getaway coming up, and he told everyone how to enlist and join along in a weekend of prayer and peace and thought in the Pacific North woods.

The week came and went. For three days, Sunday, Wednesday and Thursday night, William took names, numbers and money from his flock. Buses were ordered and food was gifted. On Thursday night after service, as people wrapped up their goodbyes and hugs, three busloads of people gathered and found their seats as the long nighttime drive began. Through dark and twisted mountain roads, towering and looming trees began to almost overgrow the highways. The buses were filled with song and sleep, with prayer and spirited discussion.

Sometime after a stint, six to seven hours maybe, the buses pulled off the long-forested highways and onto a longer more off the beaten path. Another hour and the caravan stopped at an old wrought iron gate. A series of lanterns lit the path beyond the gate, and a groundskeeper opened the gateway as the buses drove through. Now they were at Fairaway Camp.

Half a mile of dirt road and the buses made their final stop as the doors opened into the chilly night air, and the half-sleepy guests stepped out into the brisk night. Bags were collected from the transport, and a detailed map of the area was handed out to everyone. Lanterns and lampposts added the soft but effective lighting, and each cabin had a porch light. William walked every group to their cabin and said a small prayer, and when the door to the final cabin was closed, he walked off into the dark, past the lake and past the last building of the camp. The glow of the lights faded behind him. The night sounds of the wood grew as he produced a small flashlight and followed a path that was marked at the base of trees, a small symbol unnoticeable unless you knew what to look for and where to look for it. William soon found himself standing at a small wooden hut. He opened the door and saw a table, a chair and a basic bed.

William slid the table to the side and pulled back the rug, revealing a trapdoor. He opened it and climbed down the staircase.

Now he was in cold lowlight tunnels. William followed a string of shitty flickering low-energy light bulbs. After a few minutes of walking through the tunnel, he heard the low rumble of chatter and small talk. A large wooden door that looked like it was from another time was at the end of the tunnel. William opened it and he was greeted warmly by Leeland.

"Ah, my son – welcome, welcome." The two men hugged. "Gentlemen, I need not introduce William to you." Leeland turned to William. "I'm sure you remember everyone as well." Leeland motioned to a chair.

The room was fairly large with a huge oak table in the middle, chairs all around, and wine bottles; paintings from various ages hung on the wall. A large cross covered another wall. William sat down as the seven other men all shook his hand and made small talk.

These were Leeland's inner circle, the investors who had allowed Leeland access to his travels and contacts on the promise he would recover the paw. Time had been long and now the time had come.

Leeland stood up from his chair and raised a hand to silence them.

"I'm sure you're all finally ready to see it. I won't make some speech about the travels or places, the money and energy spent." Leeland reached under the table and pulled up the ornate box. The men, including William, seemed to pause and admire the box itself. Leeland opened it and placed the paw before them on the table. "Gentlemen, this is our gateway to the Lord, our gateway to salvation."

"Leeland," a voice spoke. It was old and gruff. The man who controlled this voice was David Norrel, a whale in the gas and power industry. "While I appreciate your delivery and success of your promise, why all the theatrics? You bring us all the way out into the woods. Even young William here brings members of the church. What has inspired you – if I can call it that to waste our time now with all the dressing?"

Leeland took a moment. "David, you've known me for decades now. Have I ever let you down? Do you think I'd be doing this if I didn't have a reason? Do any of you think this is all for something other than reason?" Leeland grabbed the paw and held it. "I made a wish the first time I laid my hands on it. Do you know what happened? Nothing. Nothing happened."

"So, it was a legend." Norrel said.

"I don't believe so, David. I believe it's like any source of power, a battery if you will. It simply needs a recharge. Think about it. How many eons have we tracked the timeline of the paw? I believe that while the divine rages through the paw, it also now sleeps and waits for a divine act of true righteousness and devout prayer. We must bleed as it has bled."

Leeland stood up and left the paw on the table. Walking over to a large chest of drawers, he opened one of the units and took out several cat-o-nine-tails. Walking back to the table, he placed the whips in the middle and took off his shirt, revealing deep and multiple scars on his back.

"Gentlemen." Leeland nodded to them. "William, you too. Let our blood and pain be a clear sign of devolution and love for the Lord."

Each man, including William, grabbed a cat and began to slam it onto their backs – each hit harder and harder, each barb cutting into the flesh and skin. Tearing and releasing the blood. As they did this, Leeland started to whip his chest, and then they began to pray.

A prayer of love and regret. A prayer of hope and forgiveness. Each man praying in their own tongue or way or with tears and blood.

Leeland sat. Feeling the blood trickle down his chest, his eyes fixed to the center of the cross. His body ached, but he didn't make a sound. He didn't shed a tear. In this room, it was clear. Leeland was the holiest man among them.

Friday morning came, and the sun shone high and rays cut through the trees. The happy campers had breakfast at the community cafeteria, and William walked through the crowd as he smiled and blessed the food and people. Today the kids could run about and play while the parents had to sit for a three-hour prayer in silence session.

After breakfast, the kids were let loose among the grounds. Some played tag. Others swam under the guidance of the camp-trained lifeguards. Some of the older kids went on a hike. The parents were led to a large church – no pews – just a big cross with lots of windows. Each person or couple was given a padded mat to kneel or sit on, and the prayer service started.

Unbeknownst to them that directly under the building for prayer was the room that Leeland and the others had drawn blood in. Leeland now sat as a series of prayers quietly played in the room, and Leeland held the paw against his chest and whispered to it. Using the prayers from above, Leeland siphoned the prayers, the hopes and wishes all to the paw along with his own.

For hours as the prayer session remained unbroken, Leeland took every second, every moment to empower the paw, to pray for God to restore his miracle to the paw and the world.

The prayer session came to an end, and as the parents left for lunch, Leeland laid on the hard ground in the very earth itself and held onto the paw as a mother would her newborn babe.

The children were brought for lunch and a family prayer session. As the church sat outside, Leeland was across the complex. He had a lamb tied to a fence post. The long glint of steel from the knife shone in the sun. Leeland walked toward the soft white lamb and petted its head before placing the blade under its chin. On the ground under the head the lamb was the paw on a cloth of white silk.

A moment's discomfort, the lamb tried to fight against the blade but fell to the ground. The blood spilled over the cloth and paw as Leeland said a prayer and kissed the top of the head of the now dead animal.

Two men walked up and began to take the body as Leeland took the paw and prayed at it, cradling it against his chest. Both soaked in lamb's blood.

Friday night was family prayer and games night, a sort of social mixer with some moral fiber behind it.

William led the church in song and prayer; the kids sang their songs and put on small skits from the bible. William then paused the activity for a moment as the special dinner was wheeled out.

Lamb chops, mutton and Sheppard's pie. To eat as the old world once did. The parents were given wine and the children were given sparkling grape juice.

From a far and in the cool night as the campfires lit the area and the light bounced off the lake, Leeland sat with the paw cleaning in with fresh water, taking time to make it like new. In a day and a half, the paw hadn't changed. It had been shown more love and care. More thought had been given to it and more respect had been shown to it than ever before.

"Not enough." Leeland recited to himself. The paw had been used and abused by selfish humankind for so long. "Not enough," Leeland said again.

Saturday morning, the sun rose and once again those rays cut through the trees and blessed the land. After breakfast, the church split into groups for team-based games and community building. During one of the games that took place in the woods, William and a girl snuck off. William led her down the pathway to the cabin; down into the tunnel, she would follow him anywhere.

William held her hand and walked her into the room with the cross on the wall, but the table had been made to look like a bed. They began to kiss. He undressed her. From under the table, Leeland lay there with the paw pressed against the wood, as close to them as he could get without being seen or heard. He closed his eyes as William began to fuck the girl. He made her say things. He made her pray to God, pray to him. Leeland gripped the paw before sliding out from under the table. He grabbed a knife and stood behind the girl. William held her hips as she straightened her back, and that's when Leeland dragged the blade across her throat. She coughed and sputtered. She cried and fell off the table onto the floor. William was covered in blood. Leeland walked over to the dying girl who tried to crawl and claw at life.

"Blessed child, allow your life to serve a greater purpose." Leeland held the paw in the air, as he placed his other hand over her eyes and said The Lord's Prayer. He recited this over and over as the girl lay bleeding out. William stood up, got dressed and hurried back to the woods to swim in the lake and clean off the blood before anyone noticed she was gone.

That night, the church was split into boys and girls, then men and boys and women and girls. This way was to have some bonding time within peer groups under the eyes of the camp supervision.

In a shack far away from the camp, Leeland sat with a lamp, a table and the paw. He read the bible to it. On the wall in front of him, tied to a cross, was a child, a boy about the age of ten. He had been zip tied to the cross. The chloroform was wearing off, but the gag was strong. Leeland watched the boy struggle and panic before he raised a hand. "Relax boy. You've been given a gift, a gift of the Lord – to bleed as the Lord bled, to walk in the Lord's path." Leeland opened up a tool box and took out a smaller mallet along with three very large nails.

The boy cried; he struggled against the ties.

Leeland placed a nail at the boy's wrist. "They say our Lord was hung by the hands, but this is not so. There's only meat, flesh there. Over three days the Lord would have slipped through the nail as it would have carved its way through his hand. It was the wrist." With that, Leeland slammed the first nail through the boy's wrist under the bone to hang it. The child screamed through the gag but only a muffle came through.

"You're such a brave child. Our Lord will welcome you into his kingdom with open arms." Leeland placed the other nail on the other wrist and slammed the mallet down on it. Another surge of movement and unbearable pain shot through the young body. Then Leeland took the boy's feet and placed one over the other.

The final nail was directly over the middle of them. Leeland looked into the child's eyes before driving deep into the feet. The boy writhed in pain. No one could hear him.

Leeland then dropped the mallet and took the paw. He kneeled before the dying boy, closed his eyes and prayed, clutching the paw in his hands. Hours went by as the boy tried to struggle. He'd pass out and wake up, always seeing Leeland kneeling and mumbling.

Soon the boy didn't wake. He didn't stir. Leeland locked the door and left.

Early Sunday morning before questions of the missing child and girl could be asked, every member was given wine to drink. They were gathered in the prayer hall which sat directly on top of the room where so many rituals had been done. Now Leeland and the men drank deep of their cups, and William led the church above to drink of their cups. The group started to pray. Some started to shake with the spirit or speak in tongues. They fell to the floor and writhed, and they shook and sprayed vomit and white foam from their mouths.

William left the hall.

Back down the tunnel and into the room, there with the paw sat Leeland, among dead men.

William opened the door to the scene and stood frozen.

"How did I survive?" William was angry, scared.

"Luck or your blessed I assume." Leeland said. He sat cradling the paw.

"You killed them all. you didn't even tell me!" William responded.

Leeland looked at him. "No, you were supposed to go with them young William, as you do now."

William went to rush but a shot rang out and stopped William in his tracks. Dead.

Leeland stood up and placed a gun on the table, as William dropped to the floor, holding his stomach.

"You think this has been easy? You haven't a clue to what I have done, the things I have done for this." He shook the paw.

"I have been devout. I have been honorable, and for years I allowed myself to get lost in the books and understanding. I walked the earth without a name, without a cent to my name or title. I was a beggar, a wanderer. I had thrown myself into rose bushes for lustful thoughts. I had lived with the monks. I had sat alone in prayer for two years. I had done this all and more." Leeland looked down at the body of William.

"I created you, this, all this. All to find this." Leeland shook the paw again. "I have done ungodly things such as the angels did, such as the

Old Testament told me to. I have taken the old and new books and acted, lived and became as both. I am on the precipice of greatness, and you think your plans or life are more than that of our God?"

Leeland held the paw and left the room. He walked back through the tunnel and up into the world. He walked into the center of the prayer hall among the dead and held the paw at the cross. Closing his eyes, Leeland said a prayer.

"Oh Lord, allow me to gaze upon your visage. Allow me to hear your voice. Allow me to, if only for a moment, bask in your true unchallenged divinity."

Suddenly, Leeland dropped the paw. It rattled like a snake. It shook in his hands. Leeland wide-eyed stared at the paw as a blinding white light began to flood the hall.

The sound of trumpets filled the area. They seemed to come from everywhere.

Leeland stood up and raised his arms as a figure started to appear from the light.

"Oh Lord, I am your humble servant. I am your clay. Mold me to your whim."

Leeland's love turned to terror. As from the white light, the figure came into view. A snake-headed, angel-winged creature slithered into the hall. It had six chapped udders and let out a thundering hiss.

Leeland tried to run but was caught in the tail of the creature. He tried to scream but was cut off by the dark of the God's mouth. It bit Leeland's head off and consumed his body.

Then there was silence.

Fairaway Camp was closed, and after a month of horrifying discoveries, police were able to tell what they thought was the full story.

Just another crazy suicide cult following and being destroyed by its own rituals and ego.

Police had placed everything in bags or boxes and labeled it for the evidence room. One young rookie was carrying the most out-of-place object they found.

An old withered monkey's paw.

"Man, I wish I never had to see anything like this shit again…" He dropped the paw.

"Hey, Carson – careful with that. It's evidence," said an older officer.

"It wasn't me. I swear that thing moved."

FIN

Made in United States
Troutdale, OR
04/26/2024